Welc...

Nestled on the rugg... ...que town of Penhally. ...ndy beaches, breathtaking landscapes and a warm, bustling community—it is the lucky tourist who stumbles upon this little haven.

But now Mills & Boon® Medical™ Romance is giving readers the unique opportunity to visit this fictional coastal town through our brand-new twelve-book continuity… You are welcomed to a town where the fishing boats bob up and down in the bay, surfers wait expectantly for the waves, friendly faces line the cobbled streets and romance flutters on the Cornish sea breeze…

We introduce you to Penhally Bay Surgery, where you can meet the team led by caring and commanding Dr Nick Tremayne. Each book will bring you an emotional, tempting romance—from Mediterranean heroes to a sheikh with a guarded heart. There's royal scandal that leads to marriage for a baby's sake, and handsome playboys are tamed by their blushing brides! Top-notch city surgeons win adoring smiles from the community, and little miracle babies will warm your hearts. But that's not all…

With Penhally Bay you get double the reading pleasure… as each book also follows the life of damaged hero Dr Nick Tremayne. His story will pierce your heart—a tale of lost love and the torment of forbidden romance. Dr Nick's unquestionable, unrelenting skill would leave any patient happy in the knowledge that she's in safe hands, and is a testament to the ability and dedication of all the staff at Penhally Bay Surgery. Come in and meet them for yourself…

Dear Reader

Welcome to Book 8 in this exciting series set in the beautiful Cornish town of Penhally Bay—one of the projects celebrating Mills & Boon's 100th Anniversary.

Writing is a solitary occupation, so taking part in this series was a new and interesting experience for me, and it was an honour to work with fellow Medical™ Romance authors I have admired for a long time.

VIRGIN MIDWIFE, PLAYBOY DOCTOR was wonderful to write. I immediately fell in love with my hero, Oliver Fawkner, a dedicated, drop-dead gorgeous GP. Confident, wicked and fun, Oliver also has some surprising vulnerabilities. He needs a special kind of woman—one who will see past the playboy image to the man inside. Devoted to her mums-to-be, midwife Chloe MacKinnon is kind and serene, a popular colleague and a loyal friend. But issues from her past constrain her, and she believes there is no place in her life for love.

Can Oliver teach Chloe what it means to be a woman in the fullest sense of the word? And is Chloe the one to help Oliver find the love he deserves? You'll have to read on to find out!

I hope you enjoy reading Oliver and Chloe's story as much as I loved writing it. I also hope you will follow the **Brides of Penhally Bay** series, and the other special treats marking Mills & Boon's centenary year. Here's to another hundred years of the finest romance books in the world!

Love

Margaret
www.margaretmcdonagh.com

VIRGIN MIDWIFE, PLAYBOY DOCTOR

BY
MARGARET McDONAGH

MILLS & BOON®
Pure reading pleasure

With thanks to...
Joanne, Sheila and Jenny, for inviting me to be part of this exciting
project and for all their hard work and encouragement
Shelley of Web Crafters for designing me such a great website!
And D, BB and B from T…(you know who you are!)
Thanks for making this such a moving experience!!

All the characters in this book have no existence outside the imagination
of the author, and have no relation whatsoever to anyone bearing the
same name or names. They are not even distantly inspired by any
individual known or unknown to the author, and all the incidents are
pure invention.

First published in Great Britain 2008
Harlequin Mills & Boon Limited,
Eton House, 18-24 Paradise Road, Richmond, Surrey TW9 1SR

© Margaret McDonagh 2008

ISBN: 978 0 263 86332 1

Set in Times Roman 10¼ on 11½ pt
03-0708-55765

Printed and bound in Spain
by Litografia Rosés, S.A., Barcelona

Margaret McDonagh says of herself: 'I began losing myself in the magical world of books from a very young age, and I always knew that I had to write—pursuing the dream for over twenty years, often with cussed stubbornness in the face of rejection letters! Despite having numerous romance novellas, short stories and serials published, the news that my first "proper book" had been accepted by Harlequin Mills & Boon® for their Medical™ Romance line brought indescribable joy! Having a passion for learning makes researching an involving pleasure, and I love developing new characters, getting to know them, setting them challenges to overcome. The hardest part is saying goodbye to them, because they become so real to me. And I always fall in love with my heroes! Writing and reading books, keeping in touch with friends, watching sport and meeting the demands of my four-legged companions keeps me well occupied. I hope you enjoy reading this book as much as I loved writing it.'

www.margaretmcdonagh.com
margaret.mcdonagh@yahoo.co.uk

Recent titles by the same author:

BRIDES OF PENHALLY BAY
Bachelor doctors become husbands and fathers—
in a place where hearts are made whole.

At Christmas pregnant Lucy Tremayne
was reunited with the man she loved
Christmas Eve Baby by Caroline Anderson

We snuggled up in January
with gorgeous Italian, Dr Avanti
The Italian's New-Year Marriage Wish by Sarah Morgan

Romance blossomed for Adam and Maggie in February
The Doctor's Bride by Sunrise by Josie Metcalfe

Single dad Jack Tremayne
found his perfect bride in March
The Surgeon's Fatherhood Surprise by Jennifer Taylor

In April a princess arrived in Penhally!
The Doctor's Royal Love-Child by Kate Hardy

In May Edward Tremayne found the woman of his dreams
Nurse Bride, Bayside Wedding by Gill Sanderson

June saw gorgeous Chief Inspector
Lachlan D'Ancey's wedding
Single Dad Seeks a Wife by Melanie Milburne

The temperature really hots up this month—
Dr Oliver Fawkner arrives in the Bay…
Virgin Midwife, Playboy Doctor by Margaret McDonagh

In August Francesca and Mike
try one last time for the baby they've longed for
Their Miracle Baby by Caroline Anderson

September brings sexy Sheikh Zayed
to the beaches of Penhally
Sheikh Surgeon Claims His Bride by Josie Metcalfe

Snuggle up with dishy Dr Tom Cornish in October
A Baby for Eve by Maggie Kingsley

And don't miss French doctor Gabriel,
who sweeps into the Bay this November
Dr Devereux's Proposal by Margaret McDonagh

A collection to treasure for ever!

CHAPTER ONE

'SOMETHING'S WRONG, isn't it?'

Midwife Chloe MacKinnon unwrapped the blood-pressure cuff from around Avril Harvey's arm and tried to offer the anxious woman a reassuring smile. 'Your blood pressure is rather high,' she admitted, masking her own growing concern as she re-checked the notes and previous readings.

'What about the other things?' Tears glistened in Avril's pale blue eyes, while her swollen fingers nervously shredded a paper tissue. 'I've always suspected things weren't right but the people at my previous practice in Birmingham told me not to worry. They said they were normal signs of pregnancy.'

Chloe took one trembling hand in hers and squeezed gently before returning to her chair. This was the first time she had seen Avril. The woman had moved to the small Cornish town of Penhally Bay in the last couple of weeks with her husband, Piers, both determined that their longed-for child would grow up in a better environment than the inner city. But this was Avril's first baby. And at thirty-nine, being short in stature, underweight and with a history of migraines, she had a few of the risk factors that warned Chloe to be on her guard. Add in the symptoms she had presented with that morning, and Chloe was worried about Avril's well-being as well as for that of her baby, suspecting that she had developed pre-eclampsia.

'I always saw my GP at my old practice as well as the midwife.' Avril paused and bit her lip. 'Could I see one of the doctors here today?'

'We're more midwife-led here...' Chloe hesitated as fresh tears spilled down the mother-to-be's cheeks.

'I don't want to be a nuisance, and I don't mean to doubt your expertise. It's just that I don't know anyone and I don't know what to think. I'm so scared.'

Chloe smiled, wanting to put her at ease. 'I understand, Avril, don't worry. I'll ask one of the doctors on duty to see you.'

The GPs left straightforward cases to Chloe and her colleague, Kate Althorp, but if it would set the distressed woman's mind at rest to have the second opinion, Chloe wasn't going to be awkward about it. Avril was alone in a strange place and feeling vulnerable, clearly on edge, her pale skin sallow, her short blonde hair lank. Time was of the essence. All that mattered was the safety of both mother and baby.

'Thank you, Chloe.' Avril gave a weary sigh, pressing the fingers of one hand to her temple. 'I wish my husband was with me.'

'Would you like me to call him for you?'

'No, it's all right. After dropping me here, Piers had to make the half-hour drive to St Piran for a meeting at the secondary school. He's an art teacher and he'll be working there when the new term begins,' she explained tearfully. 'We were looking forward to the summer to settle into our new home first and prepare for the baby. He won't be back for another couple of hours.'

Nodding, Chloe reached for the phone and keyed in the extension number for Reception. She watched as Avril turned her head to stare sightlessly out of the window of the room on the first floor of the expanding Penhally Bay Surgery. Chloe had tilted the blinds to keep out the full effects of the merciless July sunshine and was grateful for the coolness inside the building.

'Hello, Sue,' she said when her call was answered by the head receptionist. 'I'm with Avril Harvey for her antenatal appointment. Would you ask one of the doctors to pop upstairs for a few minutes? Thank you.'

The tone of Sue's reply assured Chloe that the woman had grasped the seriousness of the situation and would respond swiftly to the request. Hanging up, Chloe returned her attention to Avril.

'What made you choose to settle in Penhally Bay?' she asked, trying to distract the woman from her worries.

'We've been here several times for weekends and holidays—we even spent our honeymoon here ten years ago.' A reminiscent smile lightened Avril's expression. 'We both love the friendly, peaceful atmosphere, and Piers finds inspiration here for his painting.'

'Cornwall has always drawn artists. One of my friends, Lauren, is physiotherapist here, and she's an avid painter, too. Some of her work hangs on the wall in the waiting area downstairs.'

Interest momentarily chased the shadows from Avril's eyes. 'I noticed those. She's very good. Piers's paintings are more abstract. He's hoping to have time to develop and sell his work alongside the teaching.'

'So your move was both personal and professional?' Chloe encouraged.

'It seemed ideal when the job came up in St Piran. We never expected to have a child after such a long wait, but when we discovered I was pregnant, we both wanted a different kind of life for our family. I don't know what I'll do if anything happens to my baby.' A sob escaping, she rested one palm over her stomach.

Rising to her feet, Chloe pulled another tissue from the box she kept handy, then rounded the desk, squatting down to put a comforting arm around Avril's thin shoulders. 'Try not to imagine the worst-case scenarios. Even if there is something amiss, it doesn't mean you won't have a perfectly healthy baby. We're going to do all we can to help you,' she said reassuringly, handing over the fresh tissue.

'Thank you.' Avril blew her nose and dabbed at her tear-stained cheeks. 'I'm sorry to be so silly.'

'You're not being silly. It's an emotional and worrying time.'

Before she could continue, a brief knock sounded and the door opened. Chloe glanced up, barely suppressing a groan as Dr Oliver Fawkner strode into the room with his customary swagger, exuding self-confidence and blatant sex appeal. Oh, no! Why did it have to be him? Dressed in dark grey chinos and a crisp white shirt, he looked cool and unruffled, the shirt's short sleeves showing off tanned, olive-toned skin and leanly muscled forearms dusted with dark hairs. Straightening, Chloe stepped round the far side of her desk, self-consciously putting a solid barrier between them.

Oliver had been working as an extra GP at the practice since mid-June as cover for the surgery's increasing workload, the busy holiday season and while Lucy Carter continued her maternity leave. No one could deny what an excellent doctor Oliver was. But for reasons she couldn't explain, he made her feel acutely nervous. He was just too…everything. Too masculine, too much the playboy, too outrageous, too sure of himself. And far too devastating in the looks and charm departments for any woman's peace of mind. Especially a woman like her. One who shied away from male attention and anything that made her feel uncomfortable.

Nothing and no one made her feel more uncomfortable than bad boy Oliver Fawkner.

'Chloe. I heard you wanted me.'

The rough-edged, smoky voice sent a shiver rippling down her spine. Despite being five feet seven, Chloe had a long way to look up Oliver's ruggedly athletic six-foot-three-inch frame before she met the gleam of amused devilment in brown eyes as sinful and dangerous to the health as the finest chocolate. Chloe forced herself not to react when he sent her a cheeky wink. The man was a rogue. And he never missed an opportunity to tease her, flirt with her, disturb her, which only made her more tongue-tied and feeling like a gauche country bumpkin.

'Dr Fawkner, this is Avril Harvey,' she said, trying to hide her uneasiness and maintain her cool professionalism as she gave Oliver the personal details he needed about their patient's age and circumstances.

Stepping forward with his trade-mark smile, Oliver shook the woman's hand. 'Hello, Avril, it's good to meet you.'

'Th-thank you, Doctor.' Avril managed a teary smile in response. 'I'm sorry to be a bother, asking to see you.'

'You are not a bother. What seems to be the problem?' he asked, and Chloe tensed as that warm, molten gaze held her captive once more.

Clearing her throat, she dragged her gaze free and stared down at the notes. 'This is Avril's first appointment with us after moving to Penhally with her husband. She is in her thirty-second week, and until now has been attending her previous practice in Birmingham for her antenatal checks.'

'They said I was worrying for nothing,' Avril commented, continuing to shred the tissue, revealing her anxiety.

'Avril's been experiencing headaches, which are not uncommon for her with her history of migraines, but she has also had episodes with her vision, including floaters. Then there is the oedema—and lack of weight gain,' Chloe explained, meeting Oliver's gaze again, glad to see he was now in full doctor mode and all signs of teasing had vanished. 'I did the routine checks today and there is some protein in Avril's urine. Her blood pressure has spiked, too. The notes show it has been irregular in the past, but while the last reading recorded was 145 over 85, two weeks ago, today it was 190 over 110, the highest ever.'

Oliver frowned with concern, squatting down beside the mother-to-be, talking quietly to her as he examined her hands and assessed the level of swelling in her legs and ankles. Gently he rested a hand on her belly, and Chloe suspected that the smallness of the baby and Avril being underweight had not escaped his attention. He was very good with patients. Chloe just wished she felt as secure and untroubled when working with him as she did with the other male doctors in the practice, none of whom affected her the way Oliver did. Her awkwardness around him disturbed her as it was not something she had ever experienced before.

'Avril, I don't want you to worry unduly,' Oliver told the woman, continuing to hold her hand. 'But I agree with Chloe that your symptoms are more serious than your previous practice believed.'

'Oh! I knew it. What's wrong with me, Doctor? Is it the stress of the move?'

Oliver glanced up and Chloe nodded for him to continue. She wasn't territorial about her role when a second opinion was beneficial, and she worked well in partnership with the GPs to deliver the best possible care to her patients. As Avril was new and nervous, and seemed to trust Oliver, Chloe was happy to take a back seat for now.

'We suspect you have a condition called pre-eclampsia,' Oliver explained, and Chloe, impressed again with his patient care, noticed how he was respectful to include her and not take over completely.

'That's dangerous, isn't it?' Avril's voice rose with alarm. 'Is my baby going to die?'

Oliver was swift to reassure her, without scaring her unduly, about the dangers to her own health, which Chloe knew was of concern at this point. 'Not if we can help it, Avril. Pre-eclampsia affects about one in ten pregnancies and is caused by a defect in the placenta.' He glanced up and sent Chloe a quick smile, inviting her to participate.

'That's right. The baby receives nutrients and oxygen from the mother through the placenta,' she explained to Avril. 'That's why it is so important to have regular antenatal checks because the symptoms don't always show up in the early stages. Today we've seen signs that you could be affected. You have protein in your urine, your blood pressure is considerably elevated, and you have swelling in your hands, legs and feet, plus the head-aches and visual problems. If we catch things straight away, there is every chance that both you and your baby will come through this without further ill-effects.'

Avril was clearly struggling to absorb all the information. She turned her anxious gaze back to Oliver. 'What will happen? Can you give me something to make it go away?'

'No, I'm sorry, Avril, but there isn't a medical cure as such.'

'But my baby!'

Chloe handed over another tissue, which the woman took in her free hand, the other one still clasped within Oliver's. 'I know it's distressing, but you need to keep as calm as you can. Chloe will refer you to the hospital in St Piran and—'

'Is that really necessary?' Avril interrupted.

'I'm afraid it is.' Oliver's tone was firm but gentle. 'They'll monitor your symptoms, keep a close eye on your blood pressure and the levels of protein in the urine. It may be that after a day or two you can go home on strict bed rest, but they will advise you what is best.'

'Once you are lying down, especially on your left side, it is possible that your blood pressure will come down. It's a question of how effectively they can keep you settled and stable,' Chloe added.

'And if they can't?' Avril fretted.

Oliver remained calm and persuasive. 'They'll do some

tests, check your blood, and they'll listen to your baby's heart with a foetal monitor. You'll also have an ultrasound to check on the condition of your baby. Depending on what they find, they may suggest you have a steroid injection to help the baby's lungs, and you may have some other drugs for your blood pressure, and maybe some magnesium. Ultimately, the best way to protect you both would be to carry out a Caesarean and deliver your baby straight away, but that is something your doctor and midwife at the hospital will discuss with you.'

'Oh, my goodness.' Tears trickled from Avril's eyes as she sat back on the chair. 'I'm only thirty-two weeks along.'

'Everything will be done in the best interests of your baby's health and your own,' Chloe reassured her.

Oliver released Avril's hand and rose to his feet. 'Can your husband come and collect you to drive you to the hospital?'

'He's already gone to St Piran. I don't know what to do,' Avril cried.

'I can take you.' Chloe glanced up from writing a note to the midwife and doctor at the hospital. 'I'm free until after lunch when I have a couple of house calls to make before my afternoon clinic. One of those calls is halfway between here and St Piran, so it won't be a problem. We can phone your husband, Avril, and have him meet you at the hospital.'

The woman sank back in relief. 'That is so kind of you. I wouldn't like to go on my own in a taxi or something. Are you sure you don't mind?'

'Not at all,' Chloe assured her with a smile.

Her nerves tingled as she felt Oliver watching her, and her gaze was drawn to his against her will. Dark eyes focused intently on her making her shift uneasily on her chair. How did he do that? What was it about this man that made her so edgy? Thick, lustrous, over-long dark hair brushed the collar of his shirt and framed a face that was far too handsome. The straight, well-proportioned nose, sensual mouth and chiselled, masculine jaw, combined with those wicked chocolate eyes to complete the playboy package...the wealthy, devil-may-care doctor who, according to rumour, loved to surf and live the high life. A life totally opposite from her own. Shaking her head to rid herself of her unwanted thoughts about him, she mustered her reserves and kept her voice controlled.

'Thank you for your assistance, Dr Fawkner.'

A knowing smile curved his mouth. 'Always a pleasure, Chloe. I'll organise an outside line so Avril can contact her husband while you write your notes for the hospital. Then I'll help her downstairs.'

Chloe wanted to decline, to send him away, but she had to place Avril's needs above her own. 'All right,' she conceded, her evident reluctance widening Oliver's smile, a boyish dimple appearing in his left cheek.

Focusing on her task, she tried to ignore the masculine rumble of his voice, followed by Avril's tearful but brief conversation as she explained developments to her husband.

'He's going directly from the school to the hospital,' Avril confirmed, once again holding Oliver's hand as he helped her to her feet.

'That's good news. Chloe, I'll take Avril down in the lift and meet you by your car.'

'Thanks.'

Chloe gathered up her things and hurried down the stairs, stopping at Reception to explain what was happening and to collect the notes for her home visits. She was ready to head outside when the lift doors opened and Oliver gently guided Avril towards the exit. Once Avril was settled in the car, her seat belt in place, Chloe walked round to the driver's side, disconcerted when Oliver followed her. She opened the door, but the light touch of his fingers on her bare arm made her jump, and she paused, looking at him in confusion, alarmed at the way her skin burned from his touch.

'Let me know how things turn out?' he asked, and his genuine concern warmed her.

'Of course. I can check in with you later.'

'I'll look forward to it.' He hesitated a moment and Chloe fought not to reveal her discomfort when he leaned across her, making her all too aware of him as he ducked his head through the open door to talk to their patient. His body brushed against hers, and she sucked in an unsteady breath, only to find herself inhaling his unfamiliar, earthy, male scent. 'Good luck, Avril. I wish you and your husband a healthy baby. Now I'll leave you in Chloe's capable hands. She's a terrific midwife—you can trust her to give you the very best care and advice.'

Chloe was still reeling from Oliver's praise when he straightened, held her gaze for an endless moment, then stroked one finger across the tip of her nose. 'Drive carefully, babe,' he instructed, his voice soft but husky, before he stepped back to let her slide behind the steering-wheel and close the door.

Fighting down a fresh welling up of confusion, trying to ignore the way her nose prickled and her arm still tingled from the caress of his fingers, Chloe strapped on her seat belt with shaky hands and started the car. She backed out of her parking space and eased onto Harbour Road. As she headed towards the curve of the seafront and the turning to Bridge Street in the centre of town, which would take her along the side of the river and out towards the St Piran road, she glanced back one last time in her rear view-mirror.

The image that stayed with her was of Oliver, hands thrust into his trouser pockets as he stood outside the surgery, watching her go.

Despite a busy surgery, the afternoon dragged by and Oliver had a tough time concentrating and putting invasive thoughts of Chloe MacKinnon from his mind.

'Keep off that leg as much as possible for the next few

days, Linda,' he advised the young tourist, having strapped up her sprained ankle.

'I will,' she promised with a rueful smile. 'No dancing for me for a while.'

Oliver handed a prescription for some painkillers and anti-inflammatories to the girl's companion, reminding them again of the best course of action. 'Rest, ice, compression and elevation. If you have any problems don't hesitate to phone or come back and see me.'

'Thanks, Doctor.' The young man grinned at him, appearing to relish his role of nursemaid to his pretty girlfriend, helping her out of the room as Oliver opened the door and followed them through Reception.

'The pharmacy is the next building along Harbour Road.' Oliver stood with them outside the surgery entrance and pointed them in the right direction. The late afternoon heat radiated off the tarmac and sunlight shimmered on the waters in the harbour opposite where fishing boats and assorted pleasure craft bobbed on the gentle swell. 'They'll sort out the medication while you wait.'

Oliver watched for a moment as his final patient of the day hobbled along beside her boyfriend, then he went back inside and, after exchanging a few words with the receptionists, he returned to his desk in the consulting room that had been made available for his use while he was there. The previous occupant, Lucy Carter, married to Ben, an A and E consultant at St Piran, and daughter of the surgery's senior partner, Nick Tremayne, was on maternity leave.

Sighing, he set about the task of updating his patient notes and dealing with the ever-present pile of paperwork, but his attention wandered in a predictable direction. To Chloe. Whose room was immediately above his own. His gaze lifted, as if somehow by staring at the ceiling he could see her, will her presence. She was all he seemed to think about these days. And she scarcely appeared to know he was alive. It was a novel and not very pleasant experience.

He had only been in Penhally Bay a short time, but he had been drawn to Chloe from the moment they had met on his first day in his new job. And he meant what he had said earlier. Chloe was an excellent midwife…the best he had worked with. He admired her skill, her kindness, the way she always went that extra mile for the mums-to-be who meant so much to her. Like today, accepting Avril's need for another opinion and putting herself out to drive the obviously panicked woman to hospital. Perhaps he had been working too long in an impersonal big city practice. His time back in Cornwall had opened his eyes again to the true meaning and enjoyment of proper community medicine.

London had been a blast. At first. He'd had the brains to breeze through medical school, had enjoyed a successful career and an active social life since qualifying and, thanks to his family's success, he'd had the money to live life to the fullest. A cynical smile tugged his mouth. There had been good times, but his lifestyle had had its downsides, too. He was tired of those who were impressed by the family name, the bank balance, the exaggerated reputation. Tired of being used. He wanted to be seen for himself, the person he was, and not for the added trappings or as a prop to give someone else a good time. He had become mistrustful, dubious of people's— women's—motives.

He had grasped the opportunity to come back to Cornwall, his home county. His family was here, although thankfully far enough away from Penhally to allow him privacy. He loved them. They loved him. They had just never understood him. Never understood his need to make his own way and not be swallowed up in Fawkner Yachts like his grandfather, his parents, his brother and his sister. It had always been medicine that had drawn him, excited him, not the family business.

Being back in Cornwall had added benefits. He could indulge his passion for surfing and jet-skiing on an almost daily basis. And already he felt reconnected, enjoying his work in a way he had not done in the cut-and-thrust impersonal world London had become for him. Having made a conscious decision to change his life, the plan had been to settle in Penhally Bay and lie low while he established himself. He had no experience of long-term relationships, had never lived with a woman, but it was one of the things he most wanted…to find a nice girl, to settle down, to have a family. Eventually. What he had not anticipated had been meeting anyone who interested him so soon. And Chloe MacKinnon more than interested him.

She was unlike anyone he had ever known. He had never felt like this about a woman before and he was wary, unsure of venturing into the unknown. In the future, he wanted something different, some*one* different, and from all he had seen and heard so far, Chloe fitted the bill in every way. Just thinking about her made him smile and sent the blood pumping faster through his veins, a curl of heat flaming in his gut.

Chloe was the cutest thing he'd ever seen. Wholesome, in the nicest way, she had an earthy, natural beauty, something she seemed completely unaware of. She seldom wore make-up—she didn't need it. Her skin was smooth, almost translucent, while her eyes, a stunning moss green, shone between long, dusky lashes. Luscious, rosy lips begged to be kissed. At work she kept the luxuriant waves of her long ebony hair restrained in a braid, knot or ponytail, but he ached to see it loose in all its wild glory, to run his fingers through it, bury his face in it, to breathe in the lingering scent of fresh apples and sunshine that always clung to her.

Restrained was a word that could apply to Chloe in general. Serene and intelligent, she had a quiet humour that appealed to him and a sense of fun that came to the fore when she was relaxed with her friends. He had seen how she devoted all her energies to her mums-to-be and to the newborns she appeared to love with passion. She would make an amazing mother. But it was her other passions that sparked his interest and made him curious. From what he had discovered, Chloe's life outside work was a closed book—aside from her loyalty to her female friends and the evenings out she spent with them, he had no idea where she went, what she did, or who she did it with.

No doubt about it, Chloe intrigued the hell out of him. She seemed so together, so content, but she was a very private person and he had found it an uphill struggle to get close to her. At first he had assumed she must have a husband or boyfriend, for sure, but he had been amazed to discover that Chloe had no one special in her life. Furthermore, she was content that way. Why? It didn't make sense that someone so lovely and smart would be alone. But it left the field open for him. Not that he was making any headway. Chloe kept her distance from him and his own uncertainties about the timing and his suitability for a relationship made him cautious about pushing too fast.

Completely without artifice, Chloe had an air of innocence about her, one that surprised him, yet soothed his jaded spirit. He was used to women flaunting themselves and making obvious advances—it came with the territory. The Fawkner name and money drew women like iron filings to a magnet. For a time he hadn't minded. Hell, he had been young and carefree, and he had made the most of the opportunities that had come his way. But he wanted something different now— he wanted Chloe MacKinnon. He just hadn't expected it to happen so soon and wasn't sure he was ready. Yet he wasn't able to keep away from her.

Not that it had got him very far. For the first few days Chloe had treated him with the same friendly professionalism she bestowed on all her colleagues, but when he had made his personal interest in her known, she had been endearingly and puzzlingly shocked. He might have found her reaction amusing had it not led to her cooling noticeably, turning formal and businesslike, and clamming up more tightly than a bank vault.

Shaking his head, he ran his fingers through his hair, an image of Chloe vivid in his mind. She had a body to die for, but she had no notion how sexy she was. Even in the short-sleeved white tunic and loose navy blue trousers she wore to work, she turned him on as no other woman ever had. Her figure was stunning. A classic hourglass shape, with lush, full, feminine curves…soft and mouth-watering. His fingers itched to touch, his mouth to taste. But he could never get within a foot of the skittish Chloe and that was beginning to frustrate him no end.

It was a new experience for him to have to work so hard to gain a woman's attention, to get her to even speak to him outside work, let alone go out with him on a date. But despite her reserve and his own caution about getting involved with someone so soon, he wanted her more and more each day. The simmering desire nagged at him, refusing him respite, and he couldn't get her out of his head. Which meant that he somehow had to find a way past those prickly defences. Especially if he ever hoped to take her to bed. The very thought of having her naked, laid out for him, those long, inky-black tresses tumbled over his pillows, that voluptuous body arching under him as he loved her, was enough to make him harder than he'd ever been and so burning with frustration he thought he might go up in flames.

A knock on his door made him jump. For a moment he imagined it was Chloe—longed for it to be her—even if she had just come to tell him how things had gone with Avril at the hospital.

'Come in,' he called, his voice rough with desire, his heart racing in anticipation.

His gaze was fixed on the door as it slowly opened and he

almost couldn't breathe as he waited for Chloe to enter his room. When he saw, instead, that his visitor was senior partner Nick Tremayne, he struggled to swallow the wash of bitter disappointment.

'Oliver, do you have a few moments?'

'Of course, Nick.' He summoned up a smile. 'What can I do for you?'

In the short time he had been in Penhally, Oliver had come to admire the older man. He was an excellent doctor, knowledgeable if a bit aloof, but there were tensions he had yet to understand, especially between Nick and Kate Althorp, the former practice manager who had returned to her career in midwifery and now worked alongside Chloe in the practice. He suspected that Nick was a difficult man to get to know, one who felt deeply but who found it hard to share those feelings, a man who shut himself off and stuck stubbornly to a rigid point of view. Thankfully, Oliver had rubbed along well with his enigmatic boss…so far.

Exuding impatience, Nick strode across the room to gaze silently out of the window before he turned and moved back to the desk. Looking troubled, Nick folded his tall frame to sit in a chair opposite, his dark hair showing signs of grey, his gaze restless as it darted around the room.

'Is something wrong, Nick?' Oliver probed after a moment.

'What?' The older man looked up in surprise, as if disturbed from his private thoughts. 'Oh, no. No, just a lot on my mind. How are things with you? Settling in all right?'

Oliver leaned forward and folded his arms on the desk. 'Very much so. I'm enjoying my time here immensely.'

'Good. I'm glad,' he murmured, drifting again as if considering something.

Waiting patiently, Oliver reflected on the snippets of gossip he had heard. He didn't know the history between Nick and Kate, but it was clear that something had happened between them recently as they were barely speaking. At least, Nick was barely speaking to Kate, Oliver amended. Kate looked stressed and unhappy, while the tension whenever the two were near each other was palpable.

'So, Oliver,' Nick said, apparently having come to a decision. He rubbed his palms together and shifted on the chair. 'I have a favour to ask of you.'

'I'll be pleased to do what I can to help.'

Nick nodded, sitting back, his expression serious. 'I noted from your CV that you've had a special responsibility for antenatal services in a previous practice.'

'That's right,' Oliver confirmed, wondering where this was going.

'I have some extra duties coming up in the next weeks, working with the town committee regarding the twinning of Penhally with a small town in Normandy. It would be of great assistance to me if you could take over my antenatal role. Just for the time being.'

Regarding his boss closely, Oliver wondered if the twinning committee thing was a ruse. He suspected Nick wanted an excuse to avoid Kate. Frowning, he considered the request. While he didn't want to become embroiled in practice politics or take sides in whatever dispute had occurred between Nick and Kate, he couldn't deny that taking on the extra duties had an appeal. Saying yes would mean more time working closely with Chloe. And the more time he could spend with her, getting to know her, easing past her defences and deciding if there was something worth pursuing, the better as far as he was concerned.

'No problem, Nick.' There was no way he was going to turn down an opportunity to be near Chloe. 'I'll be happy to cover for you.'

The older man's relief was evident. 'Excellent. Thank you, Oliver. I'll fill you in on things and if it's not too short notice, perhaps you could start by attending the next meeting with the midwives?'

'Sure.' Oliver pulled his diary towards him and opened it. 'When is it?'

'Actually, it's in about half an hour. I, um, have to leave early,' he finished, having the grace to look uncomfortable at the lame explanation.

Hiding a smile, Oliver nodded. 'Don't worry about it.'

He listened and made notes as Nick went through the salient points he needed to know, a shiver of anticipation fluttering inside him at what lay ahead. The prospect of breaking the news to Chloe and Kate that he would be replacing Nick for the immediate future was an unappealing one. He imagined that each woman would have her own reasons to be unsettled by the change. But he wasn't going to shy away from the challenge. This unexpected turn of events could work in his favour. He was wary about the timing, unsure where any relationship might go, but instinct told him there could be something interesting between them. And desiring her as he did, he now had the perfect chance to try to woo Chloe MacKinnon.

CHAPTER TWO

CHLOE watched Kate check her watch for the tenth time in as many minutes. Kate was quite a few years her senior but they had always got on well together. The friendship had deepened further since Kate had returned to work alongside her as a midwife after giving up her job as practice manager and taking a refresher course so she could resume her previous career.

'Kate, are you all right?'

Uncharacteristically fidgety, her companion glanced up and attempted a half-hearted smile. 'Fine. Fine.'

'You realise you're holding that file upside down?' Chloe asked with calm concern.

'Oh!' Kate stared at the offending object in her hands and closed it, setting it on top of the pile in front of her. 'Sorry, Chloe, I'm as jumpy as anything.'

'Nick?'

'Who else?' Kate's wry laugh was brief and without humour.

Chloe smiled in sympathy. Having only very recently been privy to details of the latest turmoil between Kate and the senior partner at Penhally, she was worried about her friend and couldn't help but be annoyed at Nick's behaviour. True, it had to come as a shock to learn by chance that he was the father of Kate's nine-year-old-son, Jem, but to her mind his reaction had been excessive and his treatment of Kate inexcusable. Given the tension that now existed between the two of them, it was unsurprising that Kate was nervous at the prospect of their weekly antenatal meeting. The previous meetings since Nick had learned of Jem's paternity had been fraught and awkward.

'Would you rather I took the meeting on my own and brought you up to date on Monday?' Chloe offered, wanting to spare her friend and colleague further distress.

Kate shook her head. 'No, my love, thank you. I have to face him and I'm not going to run away. I've known him a long time and he has his own way of dealing with things. He can be so stubborn,' she added with a sad, resigned smile.

'If there's anything I can do…'

'Actually…' Kate straightened, a frown of consideration creasing her brow. 'I hate to impose, but are you busy tonight?'

'No, I've nothing special planned.'

'You're not going out with the girls?'

Chloe shook her head. 'Not this Friday. I'm meeting Lauren at the farmers' market tomorrow morning before my lunchtime parents' class, then we're getting together with Vicky in the evening. What did you have in mind?'

'I think I should see Nick away from work, explain things from my point of view, and leave him to mull the situation over on his own.' Kate paused as if uncertain of her plan. 'It may not work, but I feel I have to try. If you don't mind me dropping Jem off at your place for an hour or so—he does so love seeing you and playing with your cats—then I could go and talk to Nick.'

'That would be fine,' Chloe agreed as they arranged a convenient time.

Chloe hoped Kate knew what she was doing. As the older woman had rightly said, Nick could be extremely stubborn and difficult. She didn't want to see Kate hurt even more. Before she could express her concerns, the door swung open and Chloe saw that Kate's surprise matched her own when it was Oliver and not Nick who walked into the room. He was carrying a tray, and Kate hurried to clear a space on the desk so he could put it down.

'I brought refreshments,' he explained with a smile, handing around mugs of tea before passing Chloe the sugar bowl and a spoon, clearly having noted her sweet tooth. She wasn't sure what to make of that. Removing the tray, he replaced it with a biscuit tin. 'I snaffled the last of Hazel's Cornish fairings, too!'

Kate smiled at him, ever gracious and polite. 'Thank you, Oliver, this is very welcome.'

Hooking a spare chair towards him with one foot, Oliver sat and reached for his own mug. He was far too close. Her stomach tightening, her pulse racing alarmingly, Chloe drew in a ragged a breath and battled the urge to edge her own chair further away. What was he doing here? And why did he always make her feel so strange?

'Any news on Avril?' Oliver asked, opening the tin and taking out one of the delicious ginger spiced home-made biscuits.

'Yes. I was going to tell you but you were still with patients.' Chloe bit her lip cursing her defensiveness. Oliver's gaze met hers, a smile playing around his mouth, and she looked away, setting her mug down to mask her trembling fingers. 'They are monitoring Avril but it is looking increasingly likely that a Caesarean will be necessary. Probably on Monday…if she remains stable over the weekend. I'll let you know when I hear anything.'

'Thanks, I'd appreciate that. Let's hope mother and baby are both fine.'

Chloe nodded, noting how Kate sipped her tea and glanced anxiously towards the door. Her friend met her gaze and then looked at Oliver. 'Nick's not coming, is he?' she asked, undisguised hurt in her brown eyes.

'No, Kate, I'm afraid he isn't. I'm sorry.' Oliver sounded sincere and understanding. 'He's asked me to stand in for him with the antenatal work for the next couple of weeks because he has extra responsibilities on the town twinning committee.'

'I see.'

Kate's smile was strained and Chloe wasn't sure which she wanted to do more…hug her friend or give Nick a piece of her mind. This was a public slap in the face for Kate but Chloe had to admit she had been surprised by and grateful for Oliver's sensitivity. It sounded as if he thought Nick's behaviour was wrong and the town twinning work an excuse, but he was polite enough not to say so. She met his warm gaze, a confused mix of emotions swirling inside her. At the moment, however, she was too worried about how Kate was feeling to concern herself with the prospect of having to work more closely with Oliver.

With evident effort and fierce determination, Kate raised her chin. 'Shall we get on, then? We have quite a bit to cover and I don't want to be late home for Jem. I have plans this evening,' she added, meeting Chloe's gaze.

'Of course,' Chloe agreed after a moment of hesitation, still concerned at the thought of Kate going to confront Nick. 'If you're sure.'

'Positive,' Kate insisted firmly.

Oliver put his mug on her desk and took out a notebook, seemingly unaware of the undercurrents. 'OK, ladies. Be gentle with me!' His cheeky wink made Kate smile, and for that Chloe was grateful. If only she herself didn't feel so awkward around him.

'We've covered Avril Harvey, one of our new patients. There's nothing more we can do there until we hear from the hospital,' Chloe began, opening the file and making her own notes. 'All being well, mother and baby will come home safely in the days ahead.'

'We'll keep an eye on them for a few weeks before handing them over to the health visitors,' Kate agreed.

Oliver concurred. 'Fine. Who's next?'

For a while they discussed their ongoing cases, including local vet, Melinda, married to GP Dragan Lovak, who was five months pregnant and maintaining excellent health.

Kate selected the next file and filled them in on one of her cases. 'I'm regularly seeing Stephanie Richards. All is going well with her pregnancy but she's twenty-two and nervous about having this baby on her own. Her boyfriend left her and isn't interested in being a father. Stephanie's in a rented flat in Bridge Street, and there's not much help from her own family so she needs extra support from us. Her baby is also due at the end of October—the same as Melinda's.'

'As far as potential problems are concerned, I have one mother showing signs of possible placental abruption,' Chloe informed them, waiting while Oliver made a note of the name and details. 'Angela Daniels had some discomfort and spotting. She was checked out at St Piran where they did an ultrasound and full blood count, plus a Kliejaur test to detect the presence of foetal red cells in maternal circulation. It was determined that the problem was mild and Angela was sent home on bed rest once the bleeding had stopped. She's in her twenty-ninth week now.'

'So we keep a close eye on her,' Oliver commented, busy with his notebook.

'Absolutely. She's on my list and she has my pager and mobile numbers in case of an emergency.' Chloe informed him. 'Angela's also having more regular checks with the consultant at the hospital. Likewise Susan Fiddick. Didn't you see her yesterday, Kate? What is the update on her?'

Her concern for the young woman evident, Kate referred to

her file. 'The breech was spotted at her thirty-six-week appointment and they tried to turn the baby at the hospital this week, the thirty-eighth. It wasn't successful and the procedure was abandoned. St Piran is predicting difficulties and have offered Susan an elective Caesarean next week. However, Susan and her husband want her to have the baby at home by vaginal delivery. While we're all for keeping things natural whenever possible, I've advised them to reconsider…there could be problems in the next week or two,' Kate warned them.

'We'll give you any help you need,' Chloe promised.

Kate smiled. 'Thanks. Let's hope they make the decision for themselves. Now, what about our new babies?'

'I understand there's a detailed newborn screening programme in operation throughout the region.' Oliver glanced up at Kate, his gaze moving to linger on Chloe until she shifted uneasily. 'Nick mentioned it now covers cystic fibrosis?'

Chloe nodded. 'Yes, CF is now included in the screen along with sickle cell disease, phenylketonuria and congenital hypothyroidism. We do a heel-prick test on the babies when they are between five and eight days old and the samples are sent to the Newborn Screening Laboratory Service in Bristol. They test the blood for immunoreactive trypsinogen. In babies with CF, this is increased in the first few weeks of life. If IRT is found, they do DNA tests. Sometimes they require a second sample when the baby is three or four weeks old.'

'So far our babies have been clear, thank goodness,' Kate added, 'but an early diagnosis means early treatment and the prospect of a longer, healthier life.'

'I've just sent samples in for three babies, including little Timmy Morrison.' Chloe paused and gave an affectionate smile. 'Beth and Jason have been waiting years for their first child.'

'Is he the baby you delivered at their home in the early hours last Friday?' Oliver asked, returning her smile.

'Yes. They were over the moon, it was very emotional.' Embarrassed, knowing how involved she became with her mums-to-be and their babies, she dragged her gaze from Oliver's warmly knowing one and focused her attention back on the files in front of her. 'Kate, what about the Trevellyans?'

'They are having a break from IVF for a month or two, but we're keeping in regular contact while they decide what to do. I want to follow this journey through with them but…'

'What's wrong?' Oliver frowned when Kate paused.

Kate sighed, wrestling with her thoughts. 'Fran and Mike are Nick's patients. So are Susan and Darren Fiddick. I'm not sure what to tell them about the new arrangements. No offence, Oliver, but some patients are going to want to stay with Nick.'

'None taken, I assure you.' Chloe couldn't doubt the sincerity in his voice. 'The patients' needs are the most important thing and somehow we'll sort this out so that they don't have to lose either you or Nick. Don't worry, Kate. I'll have a word with Nick on Monday. I'm sure that me taking over his duties is only a short-term measure.'

Kate looked hopeful, but Chloe felt less reassured that Nick would see sense. She was grateful to Oliver for trying, however. Smiling to convey her thanks, she was confused by the flare of something hot and intense in his eyes. Her alarm increased as he shifted closer. Reaching out for another ginger biscuit, his arm brushed against hers and caused an inexplicable prickle of sensation to shoot along her nerve endings. Disconcerted, she leaned away to fuss with the files again, wondering why it was suddenly hard to breathe and uncomfortably warm in the room.

'Other than the new couples booked in for preliminary appointments next week, and anything unforeseen that comes up, I think that's it for now,' she said, her voice less steady than normal.

The others agreed, and Chloe was relieved when Oliver

gathered up the tea things and biscuit tin, putting them all back on the tray and leaving the room. She immediately felt calmer and more settled with him gone.

'I'll see you later, then, Chloe,' Kate murmured, stacking her files.

'OK.' She bit her lip. 'You still think this is a good idea?'

A mix of inner pain and fierce determination shone in the older woman's eyes. 'I think this meeting proved what needs to be done. I can't let patients suffer because of Nick's displeasure with me personally. Not that Oliver isn't a great doctor, he is, but people like the Trevellyans and the Fiddicks deserve better from Nick. They trust him to come through for them. He can't abandon them because of me.'

'Just be careful.'

'I will.' Smiling, Kate patted her arm. 'Thank you for caring. Now, I'm going to put these files away and collect my things from the staffroom.'

Chloe watched her go, sighing as she rose to her feet and made her own preparations to leave. With luck, she'd have time to go home, feed the cats, shower, change and have a snack before Kate dropped Jem off. It had been another long, busy week and she was tired. She loved her job but it could be very demanding on her time and energy, and she never knew when she could be called out by one of her mothers during the night or at a weekend. Babies didn't follow a nine-to-five, five-day-a-week schedule! Smiling to herself, she gave her room a final check and then turned to leave, shocked to find Oliver blocking her doorway.

Oliver leaned against the doorframe and watched as Chloe finished tidying her desk, a smile on her face as she turned towards him. He regretted the way that smile faded, to be replaced by wary uncertainty as her footsteps faltered and she hesitated just out of his reach. Knowing faint heart never won fair lady, he pressed ahead with his plan to ask her out.

'Hi.'

'Hello.' She looked puzzled as her gaze met his then flicked away again. 'Is something wrong?'

As nervous as a teenager, he summoned a smile and tried to look more confident than he felt. 'No, not at all. I was just wondering… Would you like to come out for a drink or something tonight?'

'Me?' Amazement shone in her green eyes before she ducked her head.

'Yes, you!' He couldn't help but laugh, shaking his head at her total lack of self-awareness. Surely guys asked her out all the time? 'Why not you?'

She regarded him in silence, apparently devoid of an answer. Closing the distance between them, he couldn't resist brushing a few wayward strands of hair that had escaped her ponytail back behind her ear. This close to her, he saw the tiny network of faint scars that crisscrossed the side of her neck and dipped to her left shoulder. He'd not noticed them before. As his fingertips trailed over the series of narrow white lines, he felt the shiver that rippled through her at his touch before she froze as if in shock.

Concerned at the thought of her being hurt in any way, his voice dropped to a husky whisper. 'What happened, babe?'

'Nothing.' Beneath his fingers he detected the rapid and irregular beat of her pulse. 'An old childhood mishap.'

Oliver didn't believe her. He could tell from her evasive tone, not to mention the shadow of remembered pain clouding her eyes, that there was much more to the event that had left these marks on her satin soft-skin than she had divulged. He was alarmed because he had never felt this intensely about a woman before. Why Chloe? What was it about her that drew him? He was impatient to know all about her, but he sensed her skittishness and knew he needed to take his time with her.

'So,' he said, getting them back on track and reluctantly removing his hand from her skin, 'about tonight…'

'I'm sorry, I can't.' Her voice sounded less steady and assured than before. 'We can talk more about any patient queries you have next week.'

She thought he was asking her out to talk about patients? Frowning, he shook his head. 'No, that's not it.' Frustrated that she didn't seem to understand his intentions, he thrust his hands in his pockets to stop himself reaching for her again. 'Chloe.'

She shifted uneasily, looking ready to flee. 'I already have plans, Oliver. I need to go.'

'Sure.' He was still puzzled by her reaction but he let it go…for now. Knowing she often met up with physiotherapist Lauren Nightingale and some of their other friends, he smiled again. 'Girls' night out?'

'No. Not this time.'

'You have a date?' Bitter disappointment and a wave of jealousy coursed through him. Had his caution meant he had missed his chance? Had some other man beaten him to Chloe?

She edged around him towards the door, her movements jerky. 'Excuse me. I'll, um, be late.'

'Of course.' Swallowing a curse, he reluctantly stood aside to let her by. 'Maybe another time.'

Scowling, unsure of himself, wondering what the hell he was doing chasing after the woman when he wasn't sure he was ready to get involved, he watched Chloe hurry to the stairs and disappear from view. He had been positive she wasn't seeing anyone. Her rejection left a sour taste in his mouth and an ache inside him. Not to mention the fact she had seemed so surprised that he would ask her out at all. Why was the idea so strange to her? What was wrong with him? Did Chloe just see him as some feckless playboy, like so many other people did?

Why was he even torturing himself over her? There had always been women who wanted to be with him, but he hadn't been interested in any of them. All he could think about, all he wanted, was Chloe. Something about her drew him in. In some inexplicable way, just being around her centred him, calmed him, made him feel real. There was so much about her he had yet to discover and he sensed there was something mysterious she held inside. He wanted to know her. Wanted Chloe to trust him, to open up to him. The prospect of an evening alone wondering where she was, what she was doing…and, dammit, who she was doing it with…was distinctly unappealing.

'Oliver?'

Glancing round in surprise, he saw Kate hovering at the staffroom door. He moved to join her, thankful to discover they were alone.

'How are you doing, Kate?' he asked, concerned that she had looked pale and stressed since the upset with Nick.

'I'm fine.'

He wasn't taken in by the brave smile she sent him. 'You can talk to me. If you ever need to.'

'Thanks.' He saw her knuckles whiten as she gripped her hands tightly together.

'I'm sorry about today. About Nick ducking out of the antenatal meeting.'

'It's not your fault.' She tried another smile, no more successful than the last. 'Nick and I have to work this out between us, Oliver.'

'OK.' He'd back off…for now. But he'd be keeping his eye on her just the same.

Kate's expression lightened as she watched him. 'How about you?'

'Me?'

'I've noticed you seem smitten with our Chloe.'

'Yeah.' That was one way of putting it. Oliver sent Kate a rueful smile. 'Not that I'm getting very far. Chloe treated me with the same friendliness she does everyone else for the first few days I was here but now she's cooled and it's almost impossible to get close to her.'

Now Kate's smile was genuine. 'I think it dawned on her that you were seeing her in a way that the other doctors don't.'

'I was interested from the first moment I met her.'

'Chloe wouldn't have realised that,' Kate commented, surprising him.

'Why not? She's a beautiful woman. Men must beat a path to her door.'

Kate shook her head. 'Hardly.'

'What are you trying to tell me?'

'Just that Chloe really is as unaware and innocent as she seems.' Kate paused and rested a hand on his arm. 'Tread carefully with her, Oliver.'

He was sure there was more here than Kate was saying. 'Tell me about Chloe.'

The older woman's expression contained a mixture of amusement and caution. 'What do you want to know?'

'Everything. Anything.' He ran a hand through his hair, his frustration showing. 'I just asked her out. She turned me down flat. She seemed to think I wanted to discuss work, but…I don't know. I gather she has a date tonight, anyway.'

'Actually, she's watching my son for me while I run an errand.'

'She is? Why didn't she say so?' Oliver stared at her in bemusement. 'I know you're friends, Kate. What do you think I should do? I didn't plan on getting involved with anyone when I came here,' he admitted, sitting down and resting his elbows on his knees. 'But…well, I hadn't counted on meeting Chloe.'

Kate frowned, taking a chair next to his. 'Chloe is…'

'What?' he prompted after she paused and the silence lengthened.

'She's not like the kind of women you're probably used to mixing with.'

He raised an eyebrow at that, irritated by the way so few people saw beyond the image. Sure, he enjoyed life, he liked to have a good time, indulge in the things he could afford and which gave him pleasure and relaxation away from the pressures and responsibilities of his work, things like surfing and jet-skiing. That didn't mean he was a jerk.

'I wanted time to settle, for the community to accept *me*, not judge on rumour and gossip or the family name.' He paused, reining in his disgruntlement. It wasn't Kate's fault. He needed to earn a new reputation, a true one. 'I've noticed you and Lauren are very protective of Chloe.'

Kate's expression softened. 'Chloe is special. Be patient, Oliver. Go slowly. Don't scare her.'

'She's frightened of me?' Shocked, he stared at Kate in disbelief. He respected women, would never cause anyone harm. 'I don't understand. I'd never hurt her.'

'Not intentionally, maybe.'

'But—'

'Chloe puts up a lot of barriers and not many people get to know the real woman,' Kate explained. 'Her work is her life and that has always suited her.'

'She doesn't date?'

'No.'

Confused, Oliver studied Kate's face. 'But why? She's intelligent, beautiful, funny.'

'I know.' The older woman's smile was filled with affection and a hint of sadness. 'You'll have your work cut out to persuade Chloe. It won't be easy. But I think you'd be good for her.' She hesitated a moment, biting her lip as she considered him. 'I can't break a confidence, Oliver, and Chloe is one of my best friends. I don't know everything, but I do know that she has issues.'

'Issues?'

'I can't say more. I would if I could—and I encourage you to persevere.'

He mulled over the information. 'Issues from her past? With men?' Was that why Chloe was so skittish?

'Only Chloe can explain…if she trusts you enough.'

So, if he really wanted to take things further, he had to keep working hard to earn Chloe's trust. Patience wasn't his strong suit, not when he wanted something badly enough…and he did want Chloe. To her friends she was special. Hadn't he sensed that, too? There was something different about her. Wasn't that why he was still interested when a relationship so soon had never been on his agenda? For some reason he couldn't yet fathom, Kate saw something in him, and was encouraging him not to give up on Chloe. He had no idea where the journey would end, but for now he was along for the ride.

'Oliver, I think you should talk to Lauren. She knows much more than I do about Chloe's past…not that she'll divulge any secrets. But she might have some better advice on how to gain Chloe's confidence.' Kate hesitated, her gaze assessing. 'If you're serious about this. Chloe's not a temporary kind of girl.'

'I know that.' Oliver frowned, seeking a way to explain feelings he scarcely understood himself. 'I came here to begin a different life, Kate, to settle down. This is new to me, but I'd like the chance to get to know Chloe, to see what develops. She affects me in ways I've never experienced before.'

'Then I think you'll find Lauren and I will do all we can to help.'

A slow smile curved Oliver's mouth as hope flared inside him. He didn't imagine wooing Chloe was going to be easy, not from the subtle, mysterious hints Kate had given him. He wasn't even sure of himself, of what he was getting into. But giving up on Chloe was not an option.

Kate stood outside Nick's imposing stone built house, situated at the opposite end of the village to her own whitewashed cottage. Was she doing the right thing? She had managed to sound confident when she had told Chloe of her plans, but much of that bravado had evaporated. It was impossible to explain how hurt she was. Nick had genuine cause to be angry at the way he had found out about Jem—overhearing her confidential confession to Eloise that day at the surgery must have been a shock—but she didn't feel it excused his behaviour towards her since. Today he had taken the easy way out in his eagerness to avoid her, but in doing so he had drawn Chloe, Oliver and a host of patients into their personal disagreement, and that wouldn't do.

Having worked up a fresh head of indignation, she walked along the path to the single-storey extension where the top half of the yellow-painted stable door stood open. Inside the expensively fitted kitchen, all wood and granite and steel, Nick stood at the island unit, his back to her. Before she lost her nerve, she rapped on the door. Nick swung round in surprise, his face creasing in a scowl of displeasure, the expression in his eyes cooling, leaving her in little doubt that she was not welcome. Tough.

'What do you want?' he demanded, voice harsh.

'We need to talk, Nick.'

He folded his arms across his chest, withdrawing into himself. 'We have nothing to talk about.'

'You're wrong.' As he turned and left the room without another word, she reached over the lip of the door and opened the bottom half, swinging it open and following him into the main part of the house, finding him in the airy sitting room. 'Don't walk away from me!'

'You're trespassing.'

'For goodness' sake!' Usually slow to ire, Kate wanted to shake the man. 'How long are you going to keep this up? It isn't going to go away by ignoring it.'

Nick faced her, his scowl deepening. 'I've told you, I don't want to talk about it. I feel betrayed, I—'

'*You* feel betrayed? That's rich. For once in your life stop and think how other people might feel. How *I* might feel.' Her hands clenched to fists at her sides. 'What we did, Nick, we did together. It was a terrible time, we needed each other. Then we both admitted it was wrong and we never spoke of it again. I had the guilt of betraying James while he was out there, dying, his body never found. How do you think it was for me, coming to terms with losing my husband, discovering I was pregnant from my one night of comfort with you? What was I supposed to do? Come and tell you and Annabel about it? Or would you rather I had sprung it on you a few years later while you were going through your own desperate grief at losing your wife? When would have been the "right time", Nick?'

He looked surprised at her outburst but no more approachable. 'I don't know. I don't have any answers. What do you expect of me?'

'Nothing. Nothing at all,' she shot back, knowing she had long ago given up expecting anything from the man she had always loved but who had chosen another woman over her, a woman for whom he was still grieving.

'What about Lucy, Jack and Edward?' he demanded, naming his grown-up children. 'What do you think this will do to them?'

'I have no idea. All I do know is that they are adults, exceptional people who have their own lives and responsibilities. You can tell them or not, as you think fit. What really worries you? That they'll think less of you?'

Shoving his hands in his pockets, Nick turned away to stare

out of the window. 'My relationships with all three of them haven't been easy.'

'No.' Kate resisted pointing out that he was largely to blame for that. It wouldn't help the current situation. 'The person who most concerns me is Jeremiah. He's only a child. I don't want him hurt.'

'I repeat, what *do* you want?' he challenged, swinging back to face her, his expression fierce.

Kate held her ground. 'I have no intention of making demands on you, or of publicly outing you as Jem's father. If you would like to spend more time getting to know him until you decide what you want to do, that's fine with me, but I won't have him hurt, used or tossed aside if it gets too much.' Taking advantage of Nick's continued silence, she pressed on. 'At work, I want you to at least be civil. It isn't fair on the other staff, or the patients, that you treat me like a pariah. Today was embarrassing for everyone, especially Chloe and Oliver. And it isn't right for people like the Trevellyans and the Fiddicks that you put our personal business before their medical needs. They are *your* patients, Nick. We have to see their journeys through with them, even if you cut back some of your other antenatal work for patients not on your list. We're adults. We made adult decisions, adult choices, adult mistakes. We have to bear the consequences like adults,' she finished, the fight draining out of her.

A muscle pulsed along Nick's jaw and he evaded her gaze. They stood in tense silence for several moments until Kate could bear it no longer. Her shoulders slumped. She knew him well enough of old to know he wasn't about to unbend, not until he had time to think things over for himself. If only she didn't still care for him, if she didn't still love him, despite all their ups and downs and all that had happened in their years of friendship.

'Think about it, Nick,' she advised quietly. 'I'll see myself out.'

She was shaking, her pulse racing from the fraught encounter, as she walked back towards the centre of the village. Finally she was passing the library and approaching the cluster of six cottages known as Fisherman's Row, which occupied the last of the space before the harbour bridge and the turning to Bridge Street. Forcing back the threat of tears, she stopped outside one of the colourful old cottages and rang Chloe's doorbell.

With Jem safely occupied, kicking a ball around the small enclosed garden at the rear of her cottage, Chloe dried her hands and went to answer the front door.

'Hi,' she greeted, stepping back to let Kate enter, noticing the glisten of unshed tears in her brown eyes and the paleness of her face, presumably evidence of her recent encounter with Nick. 'Come on in. I've just made some fresh lemonade.'

'OK.'

'Jem's out at the back. He's been fine. He wore Pirate and Cyclops out in no time,' Chloe chattered on, gesturing to the two cats curled up asleep side by side in an armchair.

Kate managed a smile. 'Thanks, Chloe. For everything.'

'No problem.' Returning the smile, she poured two glasses of the ice-cold, tangy drink and handed one to her friend. 'Would you like to sit a while?'

'That would be good.'

They chose chairs by the open doors, watching Jem play outside. Chloe curbed her nosiness but couldn't help wondering what had happened when Kate had visited Nick. It seemed clear that Kate didn't want to talk about it, however. Nick was a wonderful doctor, but he could be difficult, and he was known to be rigid in his opinions. Chloe ached for her friend and the predicament she now found herself in.

Kate had recently taken her into her confidence about Nick being Jem's father and, whilst she didn't know the circumstances of how it had all come about, she knew how much her friend fretted over it and felt guilty. Chloe could understand how Nick felt at not being told before, but she could also understand Kate's point of view. Although Kate had always been staunch in her friendship and support, Nick often appeared to take her for granted and not appreciate all she did, for the practice and for him. If both of them had felt guilty for their aberration all those years ago, and then both had needed to deal with bereavement at different times, it couldn't have been easy for Kate to know what to do for the best.

'Chloe?'

'Hmm?' Feeling relaxed, she leaned back in the chair and sipped her drink.

'Why did you let Oliver think you had a date tonight?'

Surprised at Kate's question, Chloe faced her. 'I'd made arrangements with you.'

'I could easily have changed my plans.'

'But why?' She frowned in confusion. 'Oliver probably just wanted to talk about work after our meeting. I told him we'd discuss it next week.'

Kate laughed. 'That's not at all what he wanted, Chloe!'

'It isn't?'

'No, my love!' Shaking her head, Kate reached out and patted her arm with amused tolerance. 'Oliver's interested in you.'

A prickle of breathless apprehension rippled through Chloe. 'Excuse me?'

'As a woman. Chloe…' She sighed, her smile reflecting both affection and a hint of exasperation. 'I know you don't think of yourself that way, but you *are* a woman. A beautiful woman. And Oliver has noticed.'

'He can't have!'

Laughing again but kindly, Kate finished her lemonade. 'Oliver reminds me of my late husband, James, when he was that age. The whole sexy surfer image and the warm charm, but with that underlying kindness and honesty.'

'But what am I going to do?' Chloe fretted, with increasing alarm.

'It's a new experience for you, I know, but why not try it?' Surprisingly calm in comparison to her own raging emotions, Kate's voice was gentle with understanding. 'Spend time with Oliver. Get to know him. You might find you enjoy being with him.'

With the heavy weight of her past preying on her mind, holding her in chains, Chloe stared at her friend, speechless with shock. How could Kate even suggest such a thing?

'Oh, Chloe, my love!' Chuckling, Kate set down her empty glass. 'You should see your face!' Sobering, the older woman reached out and took her hand. 'I know a little about your past, but maybe this is the perfect time for you to finally put it behind you. I hate to see you missing out on such a big part of life. Outward images can be deceptive. There's so much more to Oliver. Don't judge him on rumour. He could be the perfect man to teach you to be a woman in the fullest sense of the word—the real woman you are inside—if only you would let him.'

CHAPTER THREE

'HELLO, Oliver.'

At the sound of the female voice behind him, Oliver turned from scanning the crowds at Penhally's Saturday morning farmers' market and met Lauren Nightingale's slate-grey gaze. Tall, athletic and curvy, she was attractive, with an engaging smile, her long, light brown hair glowing lighter under the summer sunshine. Excellent at her job, the thirty year old was renowned for building rapport with her patients—and, he had discovered, affectionately teased for her inherent clumsiness. Oliver had only heard good things about her, and following the interactions he had already had with her through work, he liked her immensely.

'Hi, Lauren.'

Unable to help himself, his gaze strayed past her, eager for a glimpse of Chloe, whom Kate had hinted would be here with her friend today. He felt deflated when he could find no sign of her.

'Kate was right, you do have it bad!'

'Sorry?' The teasing in Lauren's tone had him switching his attention back to her. A frown creased his brow. 'What did you say?'

Grey eyes sparkling with mischief, Lauren linked her arm through his and led him towards a haphazard collection of tables and chairs. 'Sit for a few minutes. We'll have something to drink and discuss a strategy.'

'A strategy?' Feeling he had stepped into some kind of twilight zone, Oliver's frown deepened, but he did as instructed and sat down.

'About Chloe.' A dimpled smile appeared as Lauren faced him. 'I assume she is the reason you are here?'

'You assume correctly,' he admitted, returning the smile.

Accepting a chilled fruit smoothie, he began to relax as it dawned on him that Kate must have told Lauren about their talk, and that the younger woman was possibly not averse to the idea of him dating Chloe. At least, he hoped that was what Lauren meant by planning a strategy. Again his gaze strayed around the shifting crowds of tourists and locals examining the stallholders' wares.

'I'm afraid Chloe won't be joining us,' Lauren told him, correctly reading the direction of his thoughts. 'She was paged this morning to attend a pregnant tourist staying at the Anchor Hotel.'

Trying to mask his disappointment, Oliver nodded and decided to get straight to the point. 'So Kate's spoken of my interest in Chloe?'

'She has. And however daft it sounds, I feel as protective of Chloe as some old Victorian aunt.' The warning was softened by the smile and the laughter in her eyes, but was there nonetheless.

'That's OK. I'm glad Chloe has such good friends looking out for her,' he answered calmly, hoping to allay any fears Lauren might have. 'This isn't a game for me, Lauren. I don't know what you might have heard about my past, but—'

She raised a hand and forestalled his words. 'I'm not much of a one for heeding rumour and gossip, Oliver. I take people as I find them. And I'm a pretty good judge of character. You may not have been with us long, but I like you, so does Kate, and we both think you could be just what Chloe needs. But things are not going to be straightforward,' she finished, and this time her warning sounded more serious.

'Kate mentioned there were issues, but I don't know what they are.' He met Lauren's gaze, his own sincere. 'You and Kate both say I should keep trying. What is it you think Chloe needs? And why me?' he asked, his uncertainty showing, unsure himself whether he, who had never had a steady relationship, was able to deliver what her friends believed he could. 'What can you tell me that I need to know if I'm to begin to win Chloe's trust?'

Lauren took a sip of her tangy drink, her expression thoughtful. 'First of all, Chloe doesn't date.'

'You mean she isn't dating anyone right now?' Oliver clarified, but Lauren was shaking her head.

'No, I mean she doesn't date. Full stop.'

'Ever?' For a moment he was sure he had misunderstood but then remembered Kate had said something similar the night before. 'Chloe never dates at all?'

'That's right.'

'But why?'

Lauren's grey gaze was sombre as she faced him. 'It's a long story, Oliver, and it isn't mine to tell. I won't break Chloe's confidence, no matter how much I support what you are trying to do.'

'I wouldn't expect you to. So where do I go from here?' he persisted, puzzled.

'You'll have your work cut out for you.' Lauren's words again echoed Kate's and her smile was just as sad. 'Be Chloe's friend, don't take away her choices, don't push too hard too soon.'

A heavy knot of suspicion tightened his gut. 'Someone hurt her in the past? Physically? Emotionally? Or both?' Lauren didn't reply but, then, she didn't have to. The shadows clouding her eyes as she withdrew her gaze answered his questions more effectively than words.

They were answers he found hard to come to terms with. At some time in the past someone had abused Chloe. Pain lanced through him at the unpalatable knowledge. And anger at the unknown person who'd hurt her. Various scenarios, each more disturbing than the last, played through his mind. The new knowledge explained why Chloe devoted herself to her work, ignoring her beauty and her sexuality, friendly and warm, yet always trying to remain professional, keeping up some invisible barrier. No wonder her close friends were so protective of her.

He wanted to protect her, too, but he also felt daunted. It was a big responsibility to shoulder. Was he the right man to gentle Chloe back to life? Wary and anxious, he sat back and finished his drink, a succession of thoughts running through his mind. He doubted himself, yet Chloe's closest friends had chosen to believe in him, to trust him. After his experiences in the past, it was a heady feeling, and the start of what he had come here to find…being recognised and accepted for himself.

Everything led back to Chloe, the woman who had filled his waking moments and fired his sleeping ones with erotic dreams since the moment he had met her. The idea of any other man claiming her was unthinkable. His mind was made up. He would do all he could to earn Chloe's trust and learn her secrets. To awaken her sensuality. To show her what it was like to be loved and cherished. A step at a time.

'I'll be seeing Chloe tonight,' Lauren told him, drawing him from his thoughts. 'Kate and I will do our best to encourage her to give you a chance, but the hard work will be up to you.'

'Thanks, Lauren. I'll do all I can to live up to your faith in me, to not let Chloe down.' He hoped he was up to the task, that he wouldn't fail her.

Smiling, Lauren drained her drink. 'I believe you. So, what are you doing this weekend?' she asked, and Oliver assumed the talk of strategies for wooing Chloe was over.

'Luckily I'm off duty. Today it's surfing if the waves are right, otherwise jet-skiing. Tomorrow I thought I might take the bike out and explore. I don't know this part of Cornwall very well.'

Lauren's gaze sharpened. 'You have a motorbike?'

'Yeah. My main indulgence…along with my surfboard and jet-ski,' he admitted with a rueful smile.

'I've never ridden myself, but I know a couple of popular places where riders meet up. You might want to check them out early tomorrow morning, get some tips. It would be worth your while.'

'Great. Thank you.' Surprised at Lauren's insistence, Oliver jotted down the names of the hangouts she mentioned, marking one in particular that she recommended. 'I'll take a run out there.'

'I hope you meet up with a kindred spirit tomorrow.' For a moment, her eyes gleamed with something Oliver couldn't interpret, then she was turning away and gathering her things. Rising to her feet, she brought their chat to an end. 'See you, Oliver. Good luck.'

'Bye, Lauren. Thanks again.'

Oliver watched Lauren walk away, his mind full of thoughts and fledgling plans to win Chloe round and prove to her that he could be her friend…and more, in time.

'How did things go today? Everything OK with the mother and baby at the hotel?'

In her kitchen, opening a bottle of red wine, Chloe looked up at Lauren's question and smiled. 'Thankfully both are doing fine. They're staying in St Piran Hospital overnight as a precaution as there was some postpartum bleeding. Nothing major. The baby boy is fit and healthy. Eight pounds two ounces. There is also one very scared, very confused but very proud father.'

'Did the woman really not know she was near term?' her friend asked, an incredulous expression on her face.

'No. She didn't keep her antenatal appointments or scans because her mother told her she'd done well enough in her day and she didn't believe in a lot of interference.' Chloe grimaced, pouring the wine and handing Lauren a glass.

'Thanks.' They walked out to the tiny patio at the back of Chloe's cottage and sat to enjoy the warmth of the evening. 'All's well that ends well. I'm sure she'll be more careful with antenatal care if she has another baby.'

'I hope so. She did have a bit of a shock. So did the staff and residents of the Anchor Hotel!' Chloe chuckled, then took a sip of her wine. 'Do you want any nibbles before Vicky gets here with the pizzas?'

'No, I'm fine. Thanks.'

Chloe enjoyed meeting up with her friends. Often, like tonight, they got together at each other's houses, or they went out for a meal or to the cinema, or sometimes went dancing at one of the nightclubs in nearby Rock. With Lucy, Melinda and Eloise all wrapped up with their new husbands and, in some cases, babies or pregnancies, it was Lauren, Vicky Clements and herself who most regularly met up now. Vicky, an old school friend of Lauren's, worked at her mother's hair and beauty salon in Penhally. Chloe was three years younger than both of them, and although they hadn't been close during their school days, they had known each other all their lives in the village. Their friendships had grown in adulthood. Vicky was good fun, but she was also a terrible gossip, and Chloe was careful to guard her secrets around her. Apart from Kate at work, Chloe was closest to Lauren. And Lauren and Kate were the only people who had any inkling about her past…and the way that past impacted on her present and her future.

'There must have been something in the Penhally water this last year or so,' Lauren commented after a short silence, reclaiming Chloe's attention.

'How do you mean?'

'So many people falling in love, getting married, having babies…' Lauren looked at her and laughed. 'And not necessarily in that order!'

It had certainly been a busy time for the village and its residents. Among the many happy events to take place had been the marriage of vet Melinda Fortesque to GP Dragan Lovak. Chloe and Lauren had been bridesmaids at the wedding. Former neighbours in Fisherman's Row, Dragan and Melinda had recently moved into their dream home on the outskirts of the village and were awaiting the arrival of their first baby in October.

However, it hadn't all been people getting together and living happily ever after. Lauren herself had broken up with Martin Bennett, her long-term boyfriend. Not that she seemed upset about the split, far from it. Lauren had been more contented and freer these last weeks. Which surely lent weight to Chloe's view that you should be responsible for your own happiness and you didn't need a man. She said as much to Lauren now.

'It's true that things didn't work out with Martin. We were drifting for a long time and we never would have worked, but that doesn't mean I don't want another relationship. I'm certainly not going to be celibate for ever. I'm just taking a breather because I was with Martin so long, on and off, and I want to be sure where I am and where I am going before I meet someone else…hopefully in the months ahead. I enjoy sex, Chloe. Most people do. I know you had a terrible experience and example with your parents, but it isn't always like that. Far from it.'

Chloe bit her lip. 'I know you and Kate think I'm missing out, but how can I miss what I've never known? I'm happy with my life. What more do I need?'

Her thoughts automatically turned to Oliver. She couldn't believe he had asked her out. Not that it meant anything to him. Kate had to be wrong about that. Rumour had it that he could have his pick of women—beautiful, available, experienced women. Women who were the antithesis of her. Why on earth would Oliver be interested? And why did she find him so unsettling, so challenging? She had never reacted to any other man the way she did to him.

'I saw Oliver today.' Lauren's words, echoing her own thoughts, had Chloe's gaze jerking up in surprise. 'He really likes you, Chloe. I think you should give him a chance to show you how good a relationship can be.'

Chloe shook her head. 'I'm not designed or destined to be with anyone.'

'Nonsense.'

'But Oliver…?' Confused, Chloe took a hasty gulp of her wine, a swirl of unknown and frightening emotions rampaging inside her. Her voice was mocking when she spoke again. 'The virgin midwife and the playboy doctor? I don't think so, Lauren. I'm not the sort of person to hold Oliver's interest for a second, not if he knew about me. He'd either laugh or be bored in five minutes.'

'You're underestimating him.'

'I—'

'Why not let Oliver decide for himself?' Lauren's smile was understanding, even as her words challenged all Chloe's preconceived notions. 'He might surprise you.'

Chloe remained silent for several moments, wrestling with

uncertainty. 'I'm scared, Lauren,' she finally admitted, her voice shaky.

'I know.' Her friend leaned over and gave her a gentle hug. 'But I agree with Kate. I hate to see you only living half a life. There is so much out there for you…if you would just allow yourself to take a chance. If you don't, you're allowing your father to win, to control your life from the grave just as surely as he did before.'

Chloe sat back, lost in thought, trying to convince herself that Lauren and Kate were wrong. Her life was fine the way it was—she had a career she loved, good friends, hobbies she enjoyed. How could she need more? Need something she had never known and never wanted? She had never felt sexual desire and she had no conception of missing anything. All desire and sex and love meant to her was what she had seen her father do to her mother…along with the way he had also controlled her from a young age. In her experience, giving herself to a man meant pain and domination and humiliation, just as she and her mother had endured for years.

No one knew the full horror of it. Lauren knew part of her story. She had been there to help her all those years ago when she had needed someone. Chloe would never forget the debt she owed her friend. As for Kate, Chloe had confided the basic details, but she suspected the older woman had read more between the lines. But asking her to step outside her comfort zone, to consider something she had always rejected, to awaken a part of her she didn't even know she had…? Racked with indecision, she met Lauren's gentle grey gaze.

'I don't know what to do, Lauren.'

'Take things slowly. Get to know Oliver better. Spend time with him,' her friend advised. 'How do you feel when you are with him at work?'

'He makes me confused, jumpy, on edge. I don't understand it,' she admitted.

Lauren smiled. 'That's good.'

'It is?'

'Sure. It means you're aware of him, connecting.' Lauren paused a moment, her voice serious when she spoke again. 'Nothing can change what happened in the past, Chloe, but you can change the hold that past has on your future. Think about it. You have tomorrow to yourself. Get out in the country, like you planned.' She reached out and took her hand. 'Knowing what I do about you and your past, do you think I would encourage you to let Oliver close if I didn't trust him to take care of you? He's a good man, Chloe. Nothing like your father. Let him prove it.'

Before Chloe had the chance to reply, the sound of Vicky's shrill call reached them. 'Yoo-hoo! Anyone home?'

'We're out here,' Lauren called back, giving Chloe a moment to compose herself.

Chloe watched as Lauren moved to place her empty glass on the table, but she misjudged the distance and the glass hit the edge before toppling to the ground.

'Damn!' Lauren exclaimed as the glass shattered. 'I'm sorry, Chloe.'

'Don't worry about it. I'll clear it up. Mind you don't cut yourself.'

Tutting, irrepressible Vicky Clements, short and thin and sporting a different hair colour every week—today it was bright red—stepped outside. 'Well done, Lauren, as clumsy as ever, I see!'

Chloe shared a sympathetic smile with Lauren, infamous for her mishaps, and went to fetch the dustpan and brush. Part of her was relieved Vicky had arrived, curtailing further uncomfortable discussion, but another part of her knew it was not going to be anywhere near so easy to banish the welter of thoughts churning in her mind—all of which featured the disturbing presence of wickedly attractive Oliver Fawkner.

* * *

Early on Sunday morning, Oliver rode out of Penhally Bay, past the headland, where the church and lighthouse sat, and up Mevagissey Road to the cliffs above the beach where he had surfed the day before. He always felt an intense freedom and peace when he was out alone on his bike, and this early there were few people about to intrude on his solitude.

He had scarcely thought of anything but Chloe in the last hours, turning over all Lauren had said, worrying about what she *hadn't* said but had implied about Chloe's troubled past. Preoccupied by trying to formulate a plan to gain Chloe's confidence, he followed the directions Lauren had given him as he passed the Smugglers' Inn, then turned into the country. A short while later he was surprised to find a motorbike hire and repair place called Addison's Yard in a secluded wooded setting, then it was behind him and he rode on to the hidden beauty spot Lauren had recommended. It was beautiful. A high point on a rocky promontory, it overlooked the surrounding coast and countryside.

From Lauren's description, he had expected to find a group of bikers gathering here before heading out for a day's ride, but as he pulled off the road, he could only see one other bike. The powerful Yamaha engine idled beneath him as he pondered whether to approach the rider, who sat astride an impressive-looking red Ducati, apparently enjoying her privacy.

There was no doubt that the rider was female, given the way she filled out the lightweight black and red leathers. Oliver slowly approached, wondering why the woman had her helmet on and her visor down. Surely both must hinder her enjoyment of the view and the weather. Cruising up beside her, he switched off his bike and took off his own helmet and gloves.

'It's fantastic up here,' he commented, but his opening gambit earned him only a brief nod of the head. Anxious to ensure that the woman didn't feel uncomfortable alone with him, he decided to focus on their shared interest. 'That's a great bike.'

'Mmm.' A noncommittal grunt sounded from behind the visor.

OK. Shaking his head, wondering if Lauren was wrong about the helpfulness of fellow enthusiasts, Oliver tried again. 'I'm new to the district. I was told this was the place to come to learn of some good places to ride.' His frown deepened as his companion grunted some unintelligible reply. 'Sorry, I missed that.'

The woman shrugged. Oliver looked her over, admiring her lush curves. She almost looked like… He snapped off the ridiculous thought. Of course not. His mind was playing tricks on him. But as he studied her more closely, he noted the way a curl of dark hair had escaped from under her helmet. And then he saw the tiny feather of scars on her neck below her ear, visible above the collar of her leathers. He leaned closer and a faint hint of fresh apples teased him on the breeze. No way! He rocked back, unable to believe it. Lauren had to have known! She had sent him here to find his kindred spirit, he remembered. Hot damn!

'Chloe!' He heard a muffled yelp from inside her helmet and laughed aloud. 'I know it's you, babe. Your secret is out.'

She flipped up her visor, familiar green eyes sparking with indignation and annoyance. 'How did you know it was me?'

'I'm coming to know you—and several things gave the game away.' Reaching out, he traced the web of scars on her neck with one fingertip, feeling the tremble of her flesh beneath his touch. Pausing a moment to leisurely peruse her stunning body, his gaze rose and caught the blush that stained her cheeks before teasing, 'You look fantastic. I never would have pegged you as a biker chick, though.'

Green eyes clouded before she glanced away. 'You may believe you know me, Oliver, but I'm not at all what you think.'

And from the sound of her voice she imagined he wouldn't want to know her if he learned the truth. She couldn't be more wrong. Anger at whoever had stripped her of her confidence in herself as a woman rose inside him like an unstoppable tide. He took one of her hands in both of his. Her skin was so soft, her hand strong but gentle, fitting perfectly into his larger ones. He meant the touch to be reassuring, but even this simple contact fired his blood and sent desire fizzing through his body, reminding him he had to keep a tight rein on his self-control…at least for the time being.

'Chloe?' He waited until she drew in a ragged breath and allowed her wary gaze to return to his. Then he laid his cards on the table, honestly and sincerely. The only thing he kept back was how badly he wanted to take her to bed, knowing she was nowhere near ready to hear that yet. 'I want to know you, all of you, and to be your friend. Nothing you can tell me will make me care any less about you, or not want to know you.'

She gave a shaky laugh, her anxiety obvious. 'I don't know.'

'I'm not running away, Chloe. This isn't some passing fad to me. But I'm happy to go slowly, for us to take our time getting to know each other until you feel comfortable.' Raising her hand, he pressed a brief kiss to her palm and released her, putting some space between them so she wouldn't feel crowded. 'So, how about today? Can we take a ride together?' He cursed himself for the phraseology. The double entendre hung between them but she seemed refreshingly and inno-cently unaware of the kind of ride he really wanted to share with her. Banishing his erotic thoughts, he kept his voice soft and cajoling. 'I'd love to see your favourite parts of Cornwall. Will you show me?'

She debated for an inordinate amount of time, indecision evident in those expressive green eyes. Tense, she finally nodded, her smile nervous. 'All right.'

It was such a minor victory, and yet Oliver felt as elated at this one small achievement as he would winning the World Rip Curl Super Series surfing title or the Isle of Man TT bike race. Silently thanking Lauren for pointing him in the right direction, he pulled his gloves and helmet back on, waiting for Chloe to be ready. He was still overwhelmed and delighted to discover her unexpected adventurous spirit and love of bikes. It proved that they had more than work in common—and that the fledgling feelings he'd had for Chloe from the first were worth exploring. There was so much he wanted to share with her but he had to move cautiously, both to gain her trust and to work through his insecurities about his own past. Today he had the chance to begin that process. He couldn't wait.

Far too conscious of Oliver beside her, Chloe readied herself for their ride, silently cursing Lauren whom she imagined had been the traitor who had tipped Oliver off about where to find her that morning. Her friend had been clever, she'd give her that. Oliver had been surprised when he had recognised her. She was still amazed he had done. Hell's bells, she'd nearly fainted in shock when he'd rolled in on his impressive-looking black Yamaha and taken off his helmet!

After a fun evening with Lauren and Vicky, she had gone to bed, her rescued cats, Pirate and Cyclops, curled up near her feet, but all her dreams had been filled with images of the playboy doctor who had knocked her life out of kilter in a few short weeks. Not to mention Lauren's and Kate's combined advice to give Oliver a chance.

Sunday had dawned promising another hot, sunny day, and she had left early for Addison's Yard. With little space and no offroad parking at her cottage in Fisherman's Row, she garaged her Ducati with the enthusiastic couple who owned the bike business. After a cup of coffee with early birds Roger and Jean Addison, she'd embraced the freedom her bike afforded her and had ridden the short distance to one of her favourite secluded places to think and plan her day. To discover she shared her secret passion for motorbikes with Oliver brought another rush of confused emotions.

Feeling that sinful dark gaze focused on her, she glanced up. The way he looked at her was like a caress…not that she knew what the caress of a man felt like. But Oliver always made her feel unsettled yet strangely alive. Her palm still tingled from the kiss he had so unexpectedly and shockingly placed there. She felt gauche, out of her league. There had to be any number of experienced women keen to be with him—she wasn't so blind or stupid that she didn't realise Oliver was incredibly good-looking—so why was he interested in someone like her? Maybe if he found out about her past his interest would cease, no matter what he said to the contrary.

A smile curved his mouth and she had the unnerving feeling he knew what she was thinking. 'One step at a time, babe. Let's enjoy our day. OK?'

'OK.' Chloe heard the doubt in her own voice and knew he'd heard it, too.

She flipped down her visor, cutting off his view of her face so he couldn't read her expressions any more. Filled with nervous anticipation, she started her bike and led the way into what, for her, was the unknown…spending time with a sexy, attractive man who made his interest in her abundantly and frighteningly clear. Quite what she was going to do about that, if anything, remained to be seen.

Chloe couldn't believe how quickly the day sped by, or how disappointed she was that her time with Oliver was nearly over. They'd ridden miles along the coast and inland, spending time on Bodmin Moor with its wild landscape, granite tors, standing stones and unique history. She had imagined Oliver as a typical beach boy, interested only in surfing and women, but he'd proved to be a fascinating companion, keen to learn things, sharing unexpected bits of information and, most surprisingly of all, keeping her laughing all day. They had shared a picnic lunch on the moor, spent the afternoon exploring on both bike and foot, then had enjoyed an early fish-and-chip supper along the coast before making their way home. By evening they were back in Penhally, Oliver having followed her home after she had left her bike in its secure garage at Addison's Yard.

As she opened her front door, conscious of Oliver behind her, Chloe couldn't remember when she had last enjoyed herself so much. Usually, getting out on the bike was her escape and she liked to be alone to relax and unwind, but sharing things with Oliver today had made everything even better…special. Which was a bit scary in itself. She hadn't expected to relax with him, to enjoy being with him, for him to be so thoughtful and smart and funny. But she had—and he was.

He hadn't pressed her for details about her own life but he'd been open in telling her about himself, his childhood, the pluses and minuses of growing up in a well-known and wealthy family. The self-deprecating humour with which he had related tales of his scrapes and mishaps had brought tears of laughter to her eyes. All the while, though, she'd felt sad that she had nothing similar to offer about her own time growing up. A time dominated by her father's anger, his fists, his vicious tongue.

'What are you thinking?'

Oliver's husky voice broke through her reverie. Manufacturing a smile, she shook her head. 'Nothing.'

'You look sad.' His voice gentle, he crossed the living room, closing the gap between them.

'No.' Her memories were sad but she didn't want the past

spoiling this magical day, one she had never expected to have. 'I'm fine.'

But the thoughts, having intruded, were not so easy to banish. Was Lauren right? Was she allowing her father to control her life now as much as he had when he'd been alive? Not for the first time, she wondered what Oliver would think if she was ever able to confide in him about her father's mental, verbal and physical abuse. No matter what he had said about accepting anything she told him, she felt ashamed and embarrassed about her past. And she was sure he would laugh when he found out about her complete lack of experience with men.

She knew that her years of conditioning at home with her father had caused her to shut down one whole side of herself, but she hadn't felt she had been missing anything, had genuinely never felt interest in or desire for a man. It was Oliver who was awakening those kinds of feelings within her. And she was scared. Scared to open herself up to hurt, scared Oliver would either despise her or ridicule her for her past.

She was startled from her introspection when Oliver took both her hands in his. Uncertain, she looked up and met his dark, intense gaze, aware of the way her pulse raced and her skin tingled from his touch as his fingers stroked the sensitive insides of her wrists.

'Thank you for today, Chloe.'

His smoky voice increased the feeling of intimacy and made her skittish. 'I had a good time,' she admitted truthfully, earning herself a boyish smile.

'I'm glad. I really enjoy being with you, and I'd like us to spend much more time together.'

'Why?' She couldn't hide her confusion. 'You could have anyone.'

A chuckle rumbled from his chest. 'I don't want *anyone*. I want *you*.'

'I'm no good at this.'

'You mean letting a man get close to you?' he asked, no hint of judgement in his tone.

'I don't know how to be what you want me to be.'

For a moment his fingers tightened on hers, then he released them, but only so he could cup her face, drawing her gaze to his. Dark brown eyes looked deeply into hers. His touch was warm, sure but gentle, making her quiver from head to toe. Her chest felt tight and she wasn't sure she could remember how to breathe.

'Chloe, I never want you to be anything or anyone but yourself.' He was serious, intent, sincere. 'I like you just the way you are.'

'But—' Her words were silenced as he brushed the pad of his thumb across her lips.

'I'm not going to hurt you. We'll take things as slowly as you want,' he promised, and despite her wariness and doubt she felt warm deep inside, her heart thudding against her ribs. 'Give me a chance, babe…give *us* a chance. I want you to feel comfortable, to know you can trust me with anything.'

She finally managed to draw in a ragged breath. 'Oliver…'

'Shh. One step at a time. OK?'

'OK,' she finally agreed, not at all sure she knew what she was doing, but when he smiled at her like that she took leave of her senses, and the thought of more days like today was too tempting to resist.

'Thank you.' She saw him take a deep breath of his own, as if he was relieved or something. His thumbs stroked softly across her cheekbones, his eyes darkening as he stared at her mouth. 'May I kiss you goodnight?'

Chloe's eyes widened. 'You want to kiss me?'

'I do. Very much.' The chuckle rumbled out again, his smile deepening, bringing the dimple to his cheek. 'Is that so bad?'

he teased, eyes twinkling with amusement. 'Or such a surprise? You look like you've never been kissed before!'

'I haven't.'

He laughed, clearly disbelieving her, then his expression sobered as he continued to study her face. 'Damn,' he groaned, his body tensing. 'You're serious.'

Oliver's shock was only what she had expected. She had known he wouldn't understand. How could he think she was anything but an oddity? Chloe ducked her head as an astonished silence stretched between them. At least he knew part of the truth about her now, even though it was bound to drive him away and cool his interest in a single moment. She tried to step back but his hold tightened. He tilted her head up, but she resolutely closed her eyes so she wouldn't see the mocking derision she was sure must be in his.

'Chloe…look at me.'

'No,' she murmured, hands clenched to fists at her sides.

Oliver's hands slid along her neck to burrow into her hair, his thumbs grazing the line of her jaw, tipping her chin up further. 'Open your eyes, babe,' he insisted softly, his voice persuasive, a husky whisper that seemed to reach all her nerve endings.

Biting her lip, she mustered some bravado and forced herself to meet his gaze, surprised to find nothing but kindness and caring and honesty.

'Did you think I was going to make fun of you, or walk away?'

'I don't know.' Chloe shrugged. 'Maybe. Yes.' Frowning, she searched his gaze. 'I'm not like the kind of women you must have dated.'

'No, you're not,' he agreed, and for a moment her heart sank and a surprising wave of disappointment washed through her. 'But they're in the past. They don't interest me. You're different, Chloe. In a good way. And I'm *not* walking away.' Her heart started thudding again. She opened her mouth to protest, but the fingers of one hand brushed across her lips, silencing her. 'I'm serious when I say I don't want anyone but you. I meant it when I told you we'd take things at your pace. When you feel ready to talk, to tell me about your past and why it has held you back from experiencing your full potential as a desirable woman, I'm here to listen. Until then we'll spend more time together, get to know each other, whatever you want.'

She had no idea why, but she believed him. And she felt a crazy sense of nervous excitement she had never experienced before. Trying to block out the warnings of her past, she thought of Lauren's and Kate's advice, and especially of Oliver, this day they had shared, and took a tentative step out on a limb. 'Yes.'

'Yes?'

Oliver looked puzzled and she smiled. 'Yes, you may kiss me goodnight,' she whispered, her nervousness bringing a tremble to her voice.

Chocolate eyes turned dark and fiery as her words sank in. Again his hands moved to cup her face and her own hands rose to his chest, resting there uncertainly. Even through the soft leather she could feel the rapid beat of his heart, and when she breathed in, she inhaled the subtle masculine fragrance of him. She liked it. Her whole being shook as his head lowered and her eyes fluttered shut, the breath leaving her in a rush as his mouth met hers, his lips moving gently…warm, sure and seductive. Unable to help herself, she leaned into him. The kiss lasted no more than ten seconds. It wasn't enough. Already she wanted more, wanted to do it again, wanted it to go on for ever, and she barely suppressed a whimper of protest when he slowly pulled back.

Confused, she opened her eyes, saw Oliver's smile. Then he was letting her go, and she swayed, leaning against the sofa for support as she watched him walk away. Speechless, she pressed a hand to her mouth where the imprint of his still lingered. She licked her lips, tasting a teasing hint of the unfamiliar flavour of him. At the door, Oliver stopped and looked back at her, his eyes dark and unfathomable, his voice smoky with promise.

'Goodnight, Chloe. I'll see you tomorrow. Sweet dreams, babe.'

CHAPTER FOUR

OLIVER spent a couple of moments between patients updating his notes and preparing a referral letter to the cardiac consultant at St Piran. He was troubled by the worsening angina of the woman he had just seen, who smoked, had high blood pressure, high cholesterol and a family history of heart problems. Frowning, he concisely explained his concerns and requested the consultant's opinion.

It was Wednesday afternoon, and he was still shocked by the discoveries he had made on Sunday...the amazing day he had spent with Chloe. She was everything he had imagined and so much more. But absorbing the reality that she was twenty-seven-years old and had never even been kissed was taking some time.

Knowing she was in the room above, taking an antenatal clinic, his gaze strayed upwards. So near and yet so far. She was beyond innocent. How? Why? He had told her he would give her the time she needed to trust him, and he meant it, but that didn't mean he wasn't eager to understand why someone so beautiful and together had absolutely no idea about her own body, about need and pleasure and sexual fulfilment. Chloe wasn't being coy or shy or playing a game. She was genuine—and for some reason she had never had or explored sexual feelings.

At first, from the things Lauren and Kate had implied, he had assumed Chloe had been hurt by a previous boyfriend. But that was clearly not the case. Something much more fundamental must have happened in her earlier years to have caused her to shut off a whole part of herself. She had feared on Sunday that learning the truth of her inexperience would drive him away, make him lose interest. The opposite was the case.

Far from putting him off, Chloe's innocence brought a wave of affection and a rush of possessive satisfaction that no other man had touched her. *He* wanted to be the one to awaken her desires and teach her about the pleasures of her body, to show her how beautiful and sexy she was. But he couldn't banish the flickers of doubt that nagged at him. Was Chloe right for him? Was *he* the right man for *her*? Lauren and Kate appeared to believe so and claimed to see beyond the playboy stereotype he sought to escape. Did Chloe?

Nothing in his past had prepared him for a woman like her. Yes, he was wary, but he couldn't now imagine not having her in his life. With Chloe it would be all or nothing. He needed to go on seeing her, to win her trust and friendship, but he would have to be very sure of himself and his plans for the future before he took things beyond a few simple kisses. He was getting too far ahead of himself. For now he would spend as much time as he could with her outside work…which wasn't as easy as it sounded.

As well as being on call to her expectant mothers, Chloe had several out-of-hours ante- and postnatal groups, plus a parenting class for new mothers and fathers, in which she gave general support and advice on anything from care of the newborn to breast-feeding problems. Then there was the well-woman clinic where she helped with a range of issues, including family planning and pre-conception advice. Aside from a few snatched work-related conversations at the practice, including news of the safe delivery by C-section of Avril

Harvey's baby daughter on Monday, there had been little chance to see her at all.

But tonight, all being well, Chloe was his…for a few hours, at least. And he planned on making the most of them, talking, learning more about each other, just being together so she would feel more at ease and begin to trust him. He frowned, realising how involved his emotions were becoming with this woman. Perhaps it was time to stop doubting himself, to stop worrying that this was all happening sooner than he had planned and just see where the road ahead might lead…for them both.

Oliver glanced at his watch. He loved his job, gave one hundred per cent to his patients at all times, but he was longing to be alone with Chloe and he had another half an hour to go before both their clinics ended and he could take her home. With a resigned sigh, he pressed the buzzer and prepared to welcome his next patient.

'Let me take him for you,' Oliver offered with a smile, rising to his feet to help the harassed-looking young woman who struggled to manoeuvre a double buggy into the consulting room, one child aged about two strapped in and complaining noisily, a baby of a few months held in her free arm.

'Thanks so much.' The woman gratefully handed over the baby to Oliver's care, her answering smile rueful. 'Whoever said having the two so close together was a good idea wants their head examined.'

Chuckling, Oliver balanced the baby against his chest. 'Take your time,' he advised, waiting while she parked the buggy, sat down and endeavoured to quiet the fractious two-year-old.

'Sorry about that.' She brushed a few strands of mousy hair back from her overheated face.

'No problem.' Oliver glanced at the notes, familiarising himself with the Anker family's names. 'What can I do for you today, Juliet?'

'It's Leo,' she informed him, referring to the baby he was still holding. 'He has a cold—in this weather, can you imagine!—and he seems to have trouble breathing sometimes.'

'Let me have a look at him. How long have you noticed the problem?'

Juliet bared Leo's chest so Oliver could listen to his lungs. 'Just a couple of days. I'm probably worrying about nothing, but…'

'It's always better to be safe than sorry.' Oliver gave her a reassuring smile before resuming his thorough examination. 'His lungs are clear,' he told her a short while later, looping his stethoscope round his neck. 'Everything sounds fine. And his temperature is normal. When is Leo's breathing worse?'

'Mostly when he's trying to feed.'

Oliver checked the notes once more. 'And are you still breast-feeding?'

'Yes. I really wanted to. I had trouble managing it with William, but Chloe was wonderful, helping me through both pregnancies and supporting me afterwards. I had no problems at all feeding Leo,' she explained proudly, dressing the baby again.

'Chloe's an excellent midwife.' Oliver was all too aware of how his heart had leapt at hearing Chloe's name. With an effort he forced his mind back to the matter at hand. 'The best thing to do with Leo is to put a couple of saline drops in each nostril before feeding. That will help to thin and disperse any congestion, and he should find feeding much easier. You can also try holding him in a more upright position until he is over the cold.'

A relieved smile stripped the worry from Juliet's rosy face as she strapped Leo into place beside his now silent, watchful brother. 'That's great. Thank you so much, Dr Fawkner.'

'No trouble. You have two fine sons.' He held the door open and helped Juliet guide the buggy out of the room. 'Let me know if Leo's cold doesn't clear in another couple of days, or if you have any other concerns.'

His next patient was a middle-aged man with recurrent muscular pain in his back. After prescribing some analgesia, he recommended that the man see Lauren Nightingale for some gentle physiotherapy to help strengthen his back.

'I'm willing to try anything, Doctor,' he agreed with a wan smile.

Smiling in sympathy, Oliver made a couple of notes. 'I'll see to the referral and Lauren will contact you directly. Any problems, come back and talk to me.'

As the man made his uncomfortable departure, Oliver reflected on another mixed afternoon surgery while he waited for his final patient of the day to come through. The summer influx of tourists and surfers brought an upsurge in minor injuries and illnesses. He had been taken on at the practice to assist his new colleagues in covering the additional cases on top of the usual workload of local families, farmers and fishermen. In the weeks he had been in Penhally, he had seen everything from surfboard collisions to scrapes on the rocks, weaver and jelly-fish stings, fractures, sprains, cuts that needed stitching, and had given what seemed a never-ending series of tetanus injections.

Oliver looked up and smiled as a knock on the door announced the arrival of Rachel Kenner. He had seen from the notes that the local vicar's daughter seldom visited the surgery, but one look at her frightened blue eyes told him that something serious and troubling had brought her there today. Gently he sat her down and tried to put her at ease. Slender and shy, with short blonde curls and a nervous manner, she looked younger than her seventeen years and very vulnerable.

'Hello, Rachel. Take your time and make yourself comfortable,' he said encouragingly as she shifted restlessly on the chair. 'What can I do to help you today?'

Clasping shaking hands together in her lap, she stared at him in silence for several long moments and then burst into tears.

Chloe had just shown her last mum-to-be of the afternoon out of the room when the phone rang. She returned to her desk, grimacing at the sight of the pile of paperwork awaiting her, and picked up the receiver.

'Sorry, Chloe, am I interrupting?' Sue, the head receptionist apologised.

'No, Sue, it's fine. Mrs George has just left. Is there a problem?'

'Oliver asks if you could pop down to his consulting room as soon as you are free,' Sue continued and Chloe's heart skittered at the sound of his name and at the request. She was still gathering her wits as Sue continued. 'He has Rachel Kenner with him.'

Surprise jolted Chloe from her wayward thoughts about the man whose all-too-brief kiss three days ago still left her jittery, ridiculously excited and confused. 'Rachel? OK, I'm on my way down.'

Wondering why Reverend Kenner's shy, studious daughter might need her, Chloe hurried down the stairs to the suite of consulting rooms, frowning as she knocked on the door of what had been Lucy's room but which Oliver was now using.

'Come in.'

Stepping inside, Chloe felt another burst of nervous anticipation, then she met Oliver's darkly sinful gaze. Warmth stole through her whole being. For just a moment something intense and deeply personal burned in his eyes, and a small smile played at his mouth, then he was back in professional mode, as if the private connection had never happened.

'Thanks for coming down, Chloe.'

'No problem.' She dragged her attention away from the man who had hijacked all her thoughts of late and focused on the girl who sat by the desk, tear tracks marking her pale cheeks, a pile of soggy tissues clutched in her shaking hands. Chloe's heart went out to her, and she moved to her side, slipping an arm around her slim shoulders. 'Hello, Rachel, my love. Whatever has happened?'

Her question set off another burst of sobbing. Chloe held Rachel while she cried, raising a querying gaze to Oliver who looked on with sympathetic concern.

'Rachel's come to see us because she has a problem she's not sure how to handle,' he explained after a moment, choosing his words with care. 'I said we'd do all we can to help.'

'Of course we will,' Chloe agreed robustly, giving Rachel an encouraging smile.

Oliver hunkered down on the other side of the distraught girl and offered her a fresh tissue. His kindness touched Chloe's heart. 'Rachel, do you want to explain to Chloe, or would you like me to tell her?'

'You d-do it. P-please.' Sniffing, Rachel wiped her face and blew her nose.

'OK.' Oliver moved back, giving the teenager some space. His voice was matter-of-fact and without judgement or drama. 'Rachel had a short relationship with a boy whom she thought cared about her. Now she fears she's pregnant and she's worried about telling her father.'

Chloe couldn't have been more surprised. Rachel was the very last person she would ever have imagined being in this difficult situation. Not just because she was the vicar's daughter, or even because she was shy, but because she had been so focused on her education and her dream to be a teacher. As for Rachel's father, Chloe knew how close he and Rachel were, especially since her mother had died some years ago, leaving them alone. Reverend Kenner was a kind-hearted, generous and understanding person, and Chloe knew he would stand by Rachel no matter what. Those were bridges that could be crossed after they had determined whether the teenager *was* pregnant.

'First things first, then,' Chloe decided, following Oliver's no-nonsense approach. 'We'll do some checks to make sure, but what makes you believe you are pregnant? Have you done a home test, my love, or are you guessing because you've missed some periods?'

'Both,' Rachel admitted. The crying had stopped for now, but her voice sounded thick with tears.

Chloe gave her shoulders a reassuring squeeze. 'And how far along do you think you are, Rachel?'

'F-four months.' She hiccuped, smiling gratefully when Oliver crossed the room, returning with a cool glass of water for her. 'Thank you,' she whispered, taking a few sips. 'It only happened the once. He s-said it would be all right.'

Oliver looked resigned and Chloe smothered a sigh. How many times had they heard a tale like this one? Once was all it took. 'You don't think the father of the baby will stand by you?'

'I know he won't,' she scoffed, full of hurt and scorn.

'Can you tell us what happened?'

Rachel raised her head. Her blue eyes were red-rimmed and her lower lip trembled. 'I couldn't believe he had even noticed me. I should have known better. But he told me he cared, and he was nice to me when we went out a few times. I was stupidly flattered. I'd never had a boyfriend before. They tend not to notice me because I am shy and bookish, not to mention being the vicar's daughter,' she added with a touch of cynicism.

'But this boy did notice you?' Oliver encouraged.

'So I thought…at the time.' Rachel took another drink of water and drew in a ragged breath, fresh tears spilling from between her lashes and trickling down her pale cheeks. 'But it was all lies, just to get what he wanted. He didn't force me to have sex, I wanted to by then, but it wasn't what I expected.

I didn't enjoy it.' More tears slipped free. 'He wasn't caring at all. It really hurt.'

Chloe gave her another hug and waited until the girl calmed again. 'Who was it, Rachel?'

'G-Gary Lovelace.'

Somehow Chloe bit back a retort. Damn those Lovelaces. They were a well-known problem family in Penhally, the father in prison, not for the first time, and the mother left alone with several difficult children. Gary, the eldest at seventeen, was good-looking but lazy and always in trouble. Thrown out of school, he was now unemployed and following in his father's unsavoury footsteps. That Rachel had become one of Gary's targets was more than upsetting. Judging by Oliver's expression, he hadn't yet come into contact with the Lovelace family during his first weeks at the practice. Checking that Rachel wasn't watching, Chloe shook her head and mouthed to Oliver that she would explain later. His brief nod confirmed his understanding.

'Gary never came near me again,' Rachel continued, her shoulders shaking as she sobbed. 'I tried to talk to him, to tell him about the b-baby, and he just laughed. He said being with me had been a joke, payback to my father for his do-gooding ways.'

'Oh, Rachel,' Chloe soothed, seeing the murderous look on Oliver's face, knowing he would like a few minutes alone with wretched Gary Lovelace, just as she would.

They took some time to gentle Rachel through the necessary tests and health check, confirming the pregnancy.

'Have you given any thought to what you want to do?' Oliver asked gently as he sat back down at his desk.

'Not really.' Rachel bit her lip. 'For a while I tried to pretend none of it was happening. I have so many plans for my life. I desperately want to be a teacher. But how am I going to manage with a baby? I do know that I can't get rid of it, no matter what the circumstances or why it's here.'

Drawing up another chair, Chloe sat beside her. 'We'll do everything we can to support you, Rachel, but I honestly think you need to tell your father.'

'Oh, but I can't!' the teenager all but wailed.

'Rachel, I agree with Chloe,' Oliver announced in support. 'I know it must be scary to face these things, but your father is a good man and he'll stand by you.'

Rachel ducked her head, her shoulders shaking. 'He'll be so disappointed in me. He's so wrapped up in his community work, I hardly see him any more.'

'He loves you dearly. And you love him.' Chloe rested a reassuring hand on Rachel's arm. Her thoughts strayed for a moment and she wondered what it must be like to have a good, caring father, as Rachel did, a man so different from her own. Suppressing a shiver, she pushed her memories away. 'You're going to need his support, Rachel. This isn't something you can hide from him.'

'I just don't know how to tell him.'

Chloe opened her mouth to make a promise, then closed it again and glanced at Oliver. He smiled, a glint in his eye, as if he knew what she had been about to say.

'Would you like Chloe and me to come home with you and help explain things to your father?' Oliver offered, and Chloe smiled at him in gratitude, knowing he had somehow been in tune with her train of thought.

'You'd do that?' Rachel looked from her to Oliver and back again. 'Really?'

'Of course. If you think it would make things easier for you.'

Looking young and scared, Rachel nodded. 'Yes, please.'

'All right.' Glancing at Oliver, Chloe rose to her feet. 'I'll just pop upstairs and fetch my things, then I'll be ready to go.'

Rachel clutched her hand before she could leave. 'Thank you. Thank you both, so much.'

'Do you think Rachel will be all right?'

Hearing the worry in Chloe's voice, Oliver reached for her hand and linked his fingers with hers. So much for his plans to have her to himself for the evening, he thought wryly, given the hour or more they had spent at the vicarage after driving Rachel home. Not that he begrudged helping the teenager smooth things over with her father, or answering their endless questions. He didn't. He was just impatient to have Chloe to himself as their time alone together was precious.

'Your judgement was perfect,' he reassured her now. 'Yes, Rachel's father was shocked and upset, but he's devoted to his daughter and it's obvious he's going to stand by her. The plan to involve the aunt and uncle who live in Plymouth, and who are experienced and regular foster-parents, sounds an excellent one.'

'It would be wonderful if they agree to help Rachel care for the baby when the time comes, while she continues her A levels and does her teacher training at Plymouth university,' she agreed, sounding more hopeful.

'Exactly. And in the meantime, Rachel has her father…and us.'

The smile Chloe bestowed on him turned his heart over and sucked the air out of his lungs. 'Yes. She does. Thank you for being so good with her.'

'It wasn't me, it was you.' It was no good. He couldn't wait another moment. Coming to a halt, he drew her to face him, his free hand cupping her cheek. Slowly, carefully, he placed an all-too-brief, all-too-chaste kiss on her lips. 'You're pretty special, Chloe MacKinnon.'

A becoming blush pinkened her cheeks. 'I am not.'

'Now, we could argue about that for the rest of the

night…and I'd most definitely win,' he teased, starting them walking again.

Back at her car, Chloe opened the doors. 'Do you want me to drop you at the surgery so you can collect your own car?'

'No, it's OK. I'm not on call tonight and I can easily walk to work in the morning.' He didn't intend to waste another second of time with Chloe. 'How about we pick up something to eat?'

'That sounds nice. But I have some chicken and things for a salad in the fridge. It won't take me long to put something together. If you'd like that?' she finished doubtfully.

Did she believe such a plan might be too homely for a supposed playboy like him? He'd soon disabuse her of that worry, but that she might think it brought a sting of disappointment. The shallowness and false impressions were things he had come to Penhally Bay to escape. It mattered to him that Chloe saw the real man.

'Perfect.' He stroked one finger along her bare forearm, feeling her shiver in reaction, seeing confusion and awareness darken her eyes. He smiled and withdrew his touch. 'Thank you for asking me. I'd love to spend some quiet time at home with you.'

As she turned away and started the engine, he noticed that her hand wasn't entirely steady and she sounded more than a touch breathless. 'OK.'

Back at her cottage in Fisherman's Row, Oliver insisted on helping her put the impromptu meal together. 'Tell me about Gary Lovelace,' he requested, smiling at Chloe's unladylike exclamation.

His smile faded, however, when he learned about the reputation of the family and the endless problems they seemed to cause.

'Eve Dwyer knows more about them than I do. She's a practice nurse who lives in the village, but she's currently on an agency placement in Newquay until a vacancy becomes available back here,' Chloe explained, taking some tomatoes from the fridge and beginning to chop them. 'According to Eve, Tassie, the ten-year-old girl, is the only decent one in the Lovelace family. I don't know the whole story, but the mother, Amanda, just can't cope, and Eve is involved doing what she can to help Tassie. Gary is the main troublemaker and is leading his younger brothers astray. It sounds as if he played poor Rachel ruthlessly in one of his games. I can just imagine his sick thrill at getting the vicar's daughter in trouble.' The knife sliced through the juicy tomatoes with vigour and Oliver winced at the symbolism. 'I'd like a few moments to have my say to that boy.'

'Join the queue.'

Chloe made a murmur of agreement. 'I think most in Penhally feel the same way. Oh, blast,' she finished, setting down the knife and raising her finger to her mouth.

'Have you cut yourself?'

'It's nothing.'

Concerned, he took her hand, holding it under the cold tap for a few moments. 'Have you got any plasters?'

'In that drawer.' She pointed across the other side of the kitchen and he soon found what he needed. 'I'm getting as bad as Lauren in the clumsy stakes!'

'What is it with her?' he asked, moving back and carefully drying Chloe's cut finger on some clean absorbent kitchen roll, applying pressure to stem a fresh welling of blood.

'Lauren's always been accident-prone. Why?'

Oliver shrugged. 'I just noticed she doesn't judge distances well when she's reaching for something, and she trips over or walks into things that are in shadow.'

'You think there's something wrong?'

'Probably not if she's always been like it,' he soothed, regretting having caused Chloe any concern about her friend. But something nagged at him about Lauren's clumsiness. Pushing the thought from his mind, he gently applied the plaster over Chloe's cut. As he finished, she went to pull her hand away, but he held on. 'Wait. I haven't kissed it better yet.'

'Oh!'

Cradling her left hand, pale and delicate-looking against his darker skin, he slowly raised it, enjoying the feel of her soft skin. He placed a feather-light kiss over the injured spot, lingering a moment, his gaze holding hers, before he released her.

'There we go, babe.'

'Right. Thanks.' She looked adorably flustered. Swallowing, she turned back to the counter. 'Um, did I tell you Avril Harvey might be well enough to bring her baby home on Friday?'

Oliver hid a smile at her unsubtle change of subject. 'You did. It's good news that mother and daughter are doing well. Her husband must be relieved.'

'Yes, he is.' Placing the cold chicken on plates, Chloe drizzled dressing over the fresh salad. 'And I gather you spoke with Nick.'

'He's agreed to take back his own cases, including the Trevellyans and the Fiddicks, but I'll handle any other antenatal work not on his list for the time being,' he clarified, taking the cutlery and a jug of iced water to the table.

'Thank you. Kate will be pleased. At least Nick is being civil to her at work again—if not friendly.'

Oliver would have liked to ask what the issue was about but he didn't want to intrude on a private matter between Kate and Nick, and he also didn't want to spend this time with Chloe talking about work. He steered the conversation back to more personal things and they discussed books and music, films and motorbikes while they ate their chicken salads with soft granary rolls warmed in the oven.

'That was great,' Oliver praised when they had finished.

'Would you like some ice cream?'

Carrying the plates back to the kitchen to wash them, Oliver smiled. Chloe and her sweet tooth! 'Please.'

After drying up, he leaned against the counter, watching as she spooned out two bowls of hazelnut meringue ice cream. The uniform she still wore failed to mask her womanly curves. She was so beautiful, with her clear skin, luxuriant dark hair and those stunning green eyes. His body tightened with desire. To resist reaching for her and spoiling all his good intentions to take things slowly and let Chloe set the pace, he walked into the cosy living room. Sitting on the sofa, he familiarised himself with her two rescue cats. He knew the ginger one who had lost an eye was called Cyclops, while the all-white cat with a black patch over one eye was called Pirate.

'How did you do that?' Chloe asked a few moments later, eyes wide with surprise as she watched him stroke the cats.

'Do what?'

'Make friends with Pirate. He's very wary of trusting people, especially men. He didn't have a very happy start in life.' Her words ended abruptly and shadows clouded her eyes, as if she realised that she could have been talking about her own past. Looking uncertain, she handed him a bowl and spoon. 'Here.'

'Thanks, babe.'

Before she could move away, Oliver caught her free hand and encouraged her to sit beside him on the sofa. Sensing her unease, he kept things light, giving her time to relax again. The ice cream was excellent and he said so.

'It's from the Trevellyans' herd of pedigree Guernseys,' Chloe told him, savouring every spoonful of her treat in a way that tightened his gut more by the second. Smiling, she set her empty bowl aside. 'Mike and Fran, along with Mike's brother and sister-in-law, Joe and Sarah, produce some wonderful things. I love their blue cheese. They have a great farm shop and also sell at the weekly farmers' market.'

Oliver turned to face her, using the pad of one thumb to brush across her lips and the corner of her mouth. 'Stray ice cream,' he murmured, raising the thumb to his own mouth and sucking it.

'Oliver…'

He heard the uncertainty in her voice, but also the edge of arousal, which was matched by the darkening of her eyes. As much as he needed his next breath in order to survive, he *had* to kiss her, but he didn't want to rush her or push her too far too soon. Slowly, he leaned closer, giving her every opportunity to stop him, to move away, to say it was not what she wanted. Needing to touch her, but careful not to scare her by pulling her against him and wrapping his arms around her as he so longed to do, he closed one hand loosely around her wrist. He could feel the rapid beat of her pulse, and he loved the feel of her soft skin beneath the light caress of his fingertips. His gaze fixed on the lushness of her lips. Chloe swayed towards him. He closed the last of the distance, brushing his mouth lightly across hers, feeling and hearing her gasp as he used the tip of his tongue to clean any remaining ice cream from her skin. She was so sweet, so pure. Being with her felt so right. He longed for the day he could kiss and lick her all over.

'You taste delicious, Chloe.'

With a soft moan, she pressed her lips to his, unskilled but enthusiastic…not that he was complaining. Far from it. Used to obvious women who knew what they wanted and how to play the game, Chloe was a refreshing change. He felt protective of her. Everything about her was different. He had never felt for another woman as he did for Chloe. Had never been prepared to spend so long wooing a woman. And it had never been so important to gain someone's trust and friendship.

Oliver pulled back. Raising his free hand, his fingers traced the shape of her face. Moss-green eyes opened, fringed by sooty lashes, and she surprised him by following suit, her own fingers exploring the contours and textures of his face. Just that simple touch from her set him on fire. Catching her exploring hand, he brought it to his mouth, focusing his gaze on hers, watching her reactions as he teased her palm with his lips and tongue tip, nibbling the mound by her thumb with his teeth, making her moan.

'Oliver?'

'Mmm?' Feeling the tremor run through her, hearing the huskiness in her voice, he licked tiny circles in the centre of her palm with his tongue tip. 'You like that?'

'Yes. But…'

Responding to her nervousness, he stilled, seeing her flush and glance away. 'But?' he encouraged, his heart in his mouth as he waited to hear what she was going to say, hoping it wasn't to ask him to stop.

Chloe sucked in a ragged breath. She had never known feelings of desire and need before, and she found it hard to understand what was happening to her body. When Oliver touched her and kissed her, even looked at her with that melting dark gaze, she felt strange. Tingly and warm. Excited but nervous. Needy. He brushed his fingers over her skin and her flesh burned. He kissed her, lightly, briefly, and her body quivered in a way she had never experienced before. Deep inside she felt a knot of tension, a restlessness, an ache she wasn't sure how to assuage.

Oliver had never laughed at her or made her feel stupid. Amazingly, he still seemed to want her. And he was so patient, so gentle…undeniably sexy. Her past may have caused her to shut down that part of herself, but she didn't get to be a twenty-seven-year old midwife in the twenty-first century without understanding the mechanics of sex. She talked about it every day without embarrassment. Doing anything in practice was another matter entirely, and now she had Oliver here, had discovered how much she was enjoying being with him, she didn't have a clue what to do. A self-deprecating smile curved her lips.

'Chloe?'

His husky voice drew her from her thoughts and she realised he was still waiting for her to answer his question. His fingers stroked the sensitive flesh along the inside of her forearm and she couldn't halt the quiver that rippled through her. Could she ask? Would he mind?

'I want—' Again her words halted and she cursed herself for being so nervous.

'Tell me what you want, Chloe.' He rested his hand along the side of her neck, his thumb caressing her skin, and she leaned into his touch, seeking more. 'Never be scared to say what you need. You can always ask me anything, tell me anything. OK?'

She nodded, then sucked in a deep breath. 'I like you kissing me,' she finally admitted, bringing a dimpled smile to his handsome face.

'It's going to get even better.'

'I don't know what to do. I want…' She bit her lip, seeing his gaze drop back to her mouth. She remembered how his had felt moving teasingly over hers. It wasn't enough. 'Will you show me how to kiss properly?'

'You can count on it, babe,' he promised roughly, something hot and primal flaring in his eyes, filling her with excited anticipation and a new burst of wariness as she couldn't entirely let go of the memories of her past.

Edging closer, she tentatively rested a hand on his shoulder. 'What would lesson one be?' She was surprised at her own boldness. Surprised, too, by the inner realisation that she was coming to trust Oliver to be careful with her, to not harm her.

'Chloe…' He tensed, and for a horrible moment she thought she had misread the situation and made a fool of herself. She went to pull back, but he stopped her. 'Wait.' His eyes were impossibly dark and she discovered with amazement that his hand was unsteady as he moved to brush some wayward strands of hair back from her face. 'Are you sure?'

'Yes.' Her answer was a bare whisper, a curious mix of certainty and uncertainty churning inside her.

'Slow and easy,' Oliver murmured, almost to himself, she thought. His tongue tip peeped out as he moistened his lips, and her stomach jolted in response, but he paused again, holding her gaze. 'Any time you want to stop, we stop. OK?'

Chloe nodded, sure she was going to burst with impatience if she didn't feel his mouth against hers again…now. And then he was moving, his hand slipping round to the back of her head, his fingers sinking into her hair, his head lowering to hers. She tried to breathe and found it was almost impossible. Her heart pounded in her chest. She felt his warmth, scented his enticing masculine aroma. Then his mouth met hers, firmer this time as it moved rhythmically, knowing and arousing.

She gasped as he nibbled her lower lip, then he gently sucked on it, and she thought she was going to melt. Her hand tightened on his shoulder as she tried to balance herself. The urge to draw him closer, to press herself against him was overwhelming, but he deftly took charge, retreating when she impatiently wanted to move on, keeping her on the edge, desire spiralling more and more, leaving her feeling heady and out of control.

When his tongue teased the seam of her lips, they instinctively parted for him. She momentarily froze as she tasted him, sweet but rawly male, for the first time. Clinging to him, a whimper escaped as he changed the angle, deepening the slow, thorough, strength-sapping kiss. The tip of his tongue stroked around the insides of her lips, teasing her, before dipping inside, making her want more. But when her own tongue ventured forward to meet his, he retreated, denying her quest. Far, far too soon, the kiss was over. Chloe moaned a protest when she felt Oliver withdrawing from her, breaking contact, pulling back.

Confused, dazed, she finally managed to force her eyes open and focus on his face. His small smile was pure wickedness and gave another kick to her fluttering stomach, but she was gratified to hear that his own breathing was ragged. Realising how she was clutching him, one hand gripping the fabric of his shirt on his shoulder, the other having become entangled with his, their fingers locked together, she forced herself to relax her hold. She had no idea what to say. All she wanted to know was when they could do it again. It had been amazing.

Oliver's hand slid free of her hair, grazing across her cheek before his fingertips traced her mouth which felt swollen and sensitised from their kiss. His eyes were even darker than before, heated, watchful. She wondered what he was thinking, whether the kiss had meant anything at all to him…a kiss that had completely blown her away.

Before either of them could speak, the sound of her pager intruded on the intimate, electrically charged silence. To her regret, Oliver set her further away and released her. She felt bereft without his touch. Pulling herself together, knowing someone needed her, she fumbled for her pager with unsteady hands, anxiety gripping her when she saw who the urgent plea was from.

'What's wrong?' Oliver asked, as if reading her sudden tension.

'It's Angela Daniels. My mother-to-be on bed rest with placental abruption.' She met Oliver's dark, concerned gaze. 'She's haemorrhaging.'

CHAPTER FIVE

THE THREE hours since the call to Angela Daniels's emergency had passed in a blur. Chloe sat huddled in the passenger seat of the car and glanced across at Oliver, absorbing his strong, handsome profile in the shadows of the night. He had been a tower of strength. Having insisted on accompanying her, they had arrived at the house to find Angela's husband, Will, in a state of shock and panic, while Angela herself had collapsed on the bedroom floor and was in a bad way. Chloe had focused all her attention on Angela. Oliver had summoned the air ambulance, and then had taken charge of calming Will before coming to assist her in trying to stabilise Angela's deteriorating condition.

Seeing the woman on the floor and all that blood had brought back a terrible nightmare and for a moment Chloe had frozen, fearing that the outcome of this event would be the same as the one years ago. She had been scared that she wouldn't be good enough, competent enough. But thanks to Oliver, and the rapid dash by air ambulance to St Piran in the gathering dusk, both Angela and her baby were alive. For now. Chloe doubted whether either would have survived had they been forced to make the half-hour journey to hospital by road. As it was, the helicopter had delivered them there in minutes. Whether Angela would pull through after the amount of blood she had lost, as well as crashing twice in Resus before her baby was delivered by Caesarean, remained to be seen. Having gone along in the helicopter, Chloe now felt exhausted after the drama of the evening, drained both physically and emotionally.

Walking out to the hospital waiting area, covered in blood and battered by distressing memories, she had been amazed, relieved and more grateful than she could say to find that Oliver had followed by car to St Piran and was waiting to collect her. He had taken one look at her face and said nothing at all. He'd just been there, which was what she had needed, the look in his dark eyes one of concern and compassionate understanding. When he had slipped an arm around her, she had stiffened momentarily, but then she'd remembered that this was Oliver, and for reasons she couldn't explain, she felt safe with him. Again, he had seemed to instinctively judge her reaction, and he'd kept her close as he'd led her to the car, without ever making her feel threatened or restrained.

They were nearly back in Penhally Bay now. All she wanted was to get home. Have a shower. Face her demons. After parking the car, Oliver locked up and followed her to her front door. It was nearly midnight and the street was almost deserted, just a few tourists walking along the seafront. At the end of the eastern wall of the harbour, on the promontory beyond the church, stood the lighthouse. In the darkness of night, its beam arced out across the water, warning of the dangerous rocks where the wreck of the *Corazon del Oro* lay, the infamous seventeenth-century Spanish treasure ship which still drew tourists and divers to Penhally. Turning their backs on the village, Oliver took the keys from her shaky fingers and guided her inside her cottage. Resting his hands on her shoulders, he ushered her towards the stairs.

'Up for a bath or shower, then into bed, babe,' he instructed, his voice soft but brooking no argument. 'I'll make you a drink.'

She felt she had to attempt a token protest. 'You don't have to do that.'

'I know. But I want to. Now go,' he finished, dropping a kiss on the top of her head.

Too tired and shaken to manage further disagreement, she walked slowly up the stairs, feeling Oliver's gaze on her all the way.

Oliver watched Chloe head upstairs, a frown of concern creasing his brow. He wasn't sure what but something had happened. Something other than the emergency with Angela Daniels. Chloe had been amazing with the terrified mother-to-be—calm, professional, reassuring and skilfully efficient—but there had been a shadow in her eyes, such inner pain it had rocked him. No way was he leaving her until he knew she was all right. And, hopefully, he could encourage her to talk it out, to share whatever burden she had carried tonight.

He headed for the kitchen and hunted out the necessary ingredients for hot chocolate. It wasn't the weather for it as the night was sultry after another sweltering July day, but Chloe needed something comforting. And as he couldn't take her to bed and love her into a state of pleasured oblivion, the hot chocolate would have to do for now. Waiting for the drink to heat, hearing the shower running upstairs, he leaned against the counter and thought back over the evening.

Chloe's innocent eagerness to experiment, her shy boldness in asking for what she wanted, had both delighted and encouraged him. And it had been increasingly difficult to keep a rein on his desire as he had kissed her—less chastely than before. She had been nervous but she had enjoyed it, and he had been careful to call a halt before she had been ready to stop, leaving her disappointed and wanting more. He couldn't wait for the day he could kiss her freely, letting loose all the passion and hunger he had for her. But it was too soon. That had been re-

inforced by the way Chloe had tensed when he had put his arm
round her at the hospital. Apparently kissing was one thing,
being held was something else entirely. Something he would
have to work on gently now he knew of her anxiety. Now he
had admitted to himself that, whatever his doubts, no way
could he walk away from this woman. Chloe needed someone
to coax her out of her inner prison. He wanted to be that man.
To be good enough for her. He wanted to discover what it was
that haunted her and to try to make it right.

Tonight wasn't the time to ask, but he did hope to learn what
had affected her so deeply with Angela. By the time the hot
chocolate was ready, the shower had stopped. He found a con-
tainer of tiny marshmallows and dropped a couple into her mug
to melt, then headed upstairs, unexpectedly meeting her
emerging from the bathroom. He stopped, unable to move,
scared he'd drop the drinks or go into meltdown like a marsh-
mallow himself at the sight of her dressed only in a soft, figure-
hugging, sleeveless vest top and a flimsy pair of cotton boxers
that revealed the length of her legs.

Great legs. Not too slender, but shapely and well curved. He
could imagine all too clearly how they would feel wrapped
around him as he… No, he couldn't afford to think erotic
thoughts right now. He dragged his gaze upwards, only to halt
at the delectable view of her full, firm breasts. Oh, hell. To
torment him even further, pebbled nipples pressed out the thin
cotton fabric of her top. His mouth watered. His hands craved
to be free to fill themselves with her tempting flesh. Instead,
his fingers tightened round the mugs in desperation and he val-
iantly sought to ignore the clamour of his own body as it responded to the sight of hers.

He cleared his throat, his voice gruff. 'Bed.' For a moment
he closed his eyes. If only he could join her there.

Chloe, apparently innocently unaware both of the image she
presented and his reaction, complied without comment. He

followed her into her room, knowing he had to have taken leave of his senses…and that a cold shower was going to do little to stave off the state of his raging desire for Chloe tonight. Painfully aroused, he watched as she moved to the bed, sliding beneath the single light sheet that was her only covering for the heat of the summer night. Handing her the mugs, Oliver toed off his shoes. Propping himself next to her, on top of the sheet, he accepted his mug and then took her free hand in his, waiting for her to relax before even thinking of drawing her closer.

For a while they sipped their drinks in silence. He could feel her tension—it almost vibrated off her—and it was there in the tautness of her face reflected in the glow of the single lamp on the bedside chest next to her.

'You did a great job tonight, Chloe.'

Setting her empty mug aside, she shrugged. 'It was touch and go. I was grateful for your help. I know Angela wanted to be at home but, given the signs on her last scan, it may have been wiser had she stayed in hospital.'

'That was the consultant's call. Not yours.'

'Yes. I know.'

OK, so she wasn't blaming herself for the sudden deterioration in Angela's condition, which had been one of his fears. If that wasn't the issue, what was it that had upset her? Careful not to scare her by holding her down, he leaned across her to put his mug next to hers. Moving back into place, he slid an arm around her shoulders and drew her closer, cradling her head against his chest. With one hand he stroked the loose locks of her glossy, ebony hair.

Chloe held herself stiffly against him, but he didn't move, just waited, offering comfort, revelling in being able to hold her for the first time. The fact that she hadn't immediately pulled away was a major breakthrough. Even if she wasn't actively participating.

'Relax,' he murmured, keeping his voice low. His heart clenched when she drew in a ragged breath, only for it to shudder out of her. 'You're shaking. Don't you like being hugged?'

He thought she wasn't going to answer, but when she finally spoke, he had to strain to hear her whispered words. 'I'm not used to it.'

'I hope to be doing it a lot…if you'll let me,' he told her softly, careful to keep his hold loose so she didn't feel restrained.

He wanted answers but knew he had to be calm and patient, however frustrating it might be. Until he knew what had happened in her past, he didn't know what he was working against, what could alarm her or having her backing off. He felt like he was walking on eggshells.

'You are an incredible midwife, Chloe,' he praised, returning to their former conversation.

'Thank you.' He heard the surprise and pleasure in her voice at his compliment.

'I've worked with many people in different places who "do midwifery" but you are a proper midwife for all the right reasons and in all the right ways. I admire your desire to let things develop naturally for both mother and baby, using as little intervention as possible and putting the mother first. The care here is very patient-led and holistic. It's refreshing. And it's a real pleasure to work with you and Kate. You really believe in what you are doing. It's not just a job.'

'Not to me. I enjoy what I do.'

'It shows.' He continued stroking her hair. 'What made you choose midwifery as a career?' he asked, knowing when he felt her stiffen that he had touched something raw inside her. 'Chloe?'

A deep painful sigh escaped her but she didn't pull away.

He waited, hoping she was coming to trust him enough to confide in him about something important to her.

'I came home from school one day to find my mother lying on the floor, bleeding.'

The words cut through him and he smothered a groan as it dawned on him what seeing Angela must have meant to Chloe. 'Tonight made you remember.'

'Yes. For a moment I froze, and it was as if I was reliving it.' A tremor ran through her and he instinctively cuddled her closer. 'I was ten. My mother was six months pregnant.' Her voice was flat but the underlying emotion was obvious and Oliver ached for her. 'I called the ambulance but it seemed to take ages to come. The person on the phone told me what to do, and I tried…tried to keep calm and help. My mother survived, but it was hopeless for the baby.'

So she had become a midwife, needing to do all she could to help others as she hadn't been able to help her mother? 'It wasn't your fault, Chloe,' he reassured her, his voice rough.

'I couldn't do anything. I let my little brother die.' A sob of guilt was barely suppressed at her confession.

'Chloe, you were a child. You were not responsible, not to blame,' he insisted, wanting to ease the pain she had buried all this time and which had come back to haunt her after finding Angela in a similar situation. 'With the knowledge you now have, you know that even the best professional could not have saved your brother. Sometimes these things happen, a fluke of nature.'

'He killed him.'

Oliver hesitated, not sure if she knew what she was saying, or whether the trauma the ten-year-old child had endured had made her confused. 'Who did?' He moved his fingers under her hair to soothingly massage the back of her neck.

'My father.' She sucked in a ragged breath, still tense in his arms. 'He'd gone off on one of his rages. He hit her, she fell…and he kicked her in the stomach. That's why she miscarried. He said he never wanted the baby anyway. He left her to bleed to death, wanted them both to die, and he went out fishing. If I hadn't come in and found her… Later he blamed me for saving her.'

'God, Chloe.'

This was the first real confidence she had ever shared with him. Instinctively he gathered her unprotesting form closer still, breathing in the fresh apple scent of her hair and skin. What she had told him was shocking enough, but the way she had recounted it, as if such violence at home had been nothing unusual, made him feel sick. What must it have been like to grow up in that kind of environment? And then it occurred to him that he may have unwittingly discovered the root of the problem. Was the dark spectre in Chloe's past her father? If so, it made sense that she never wanted to speak of her childhood. It seemed that every time he came closer to an answer, all he found were more questions.

Oliver couldn't bear the thought of Chloe being hurt in any way. Yet someone *had* hurt her. And the prime suspect was her father. It tore at him that she had been emotionally and physically dominated by someone who should have loved and cared for her. No wonder she didn't trust those emotions. Or men. Despite everything she had been through, she had survived and triumphed, at least in terms of her career, her friendships, her hobbies. But she had closed her mind and her heart to love, men and sex. He had yet to find out the full details of what had happened, but he desperately wanted to teach Chloe that she could trust him not to hurt her or control her, that it was safe to experience with him all the things she had banished from her life until now.

'I'm sorry,' she murmured, making him frown.

'There's nothing whatever for you to apologise for.'

She relaxed more against him. 'Thank you for being here this evening.'

'I'll always be here for you, babe.'

As he spoke the words, he knew how much he meant them. While part of him was scared of what he would be taking on by pursuing things with Chloe, he recognised that he was in too deep, his emotions and his desires ensnared, to back away and let her down. Lost in his own thoughts, he dropped a kiss on the top of her head, his free hand moving to whisper up and down her bare arm.

Something had happened to him the day he had met Chloe. Her friends said she was special and the more he came to know her the more he knew that was true. From the first moment he had been drawn to her. He thought back over the pleasant but meaningless relationships he had been involved in over the years. Most had been brief and temporarily satisfying, but had never filled a hidden void he had never allowed himself to acknowledge until recently, when the urge for a different and settled life had brought him back to Cornwall.

With Chloe, the smallest, most seemingly insignificant progress felt like the greatest victory of his life, and just being with her made him happy. Yes, he wanted to make love to her, but what he felt with Chloe, what he *needed* with her, was about so much more than sex. For the first time in his life he wanted a woman for more than a mutually enjoyable but short-lived affair. Chloe was more. So much more in every way. Yet the responsibility of all that meant weighed heavily on him. He didn't doubt his steadfastness. He wanted to settle down, to have a family of his own, and he knew that when he found the right woman, he would be loyal and faithful and loving, in for the long haul. *Was* Chloe the one? Could she see beyond the Fawkner name and the old reputation to the person he was inside?

With his mind occupied, Oliver held Chloe until she fell

asleep. Nothing would please him more than to slide under the sheet and stay with her all night, but he knew what small communities were like and he wasn't prepared to make her the subject of unwitting gossip. He wanted people here to see him for what he was now. If and when Chloe asked him to stay of her own free will…well, that was a different matter entirely. Regretfully, he eased away and slipped on his shoes. Making sure she was comfortable, he watched her sleep, his chest tight with longing and his growing feelings for her.

Turning away, he used the pad and pen Chloe kept on the bedside chest to write her a note. Leaving his message where she would find it when she woke up, he bent and kissed her lightly on the forehead before switching off the lamp and leaving her room. After checking that her cottage was secure, and that the two cats had fresh water, he took Chloe's spare keys, let himself out and locked the door after him.

He walked the short distance up Bridge Street to the flat Nick had arranged for him to rent until the end of July. Soon he would have to make more permanent plans. But even knowing he wasn't going to spend many of the few hours left of the night asleep, he couldn't think about anything now. His mind was too full of Chloe.

'I hear you had an eventful night,' Kate commented with a sympathetic smile when Chloe arrived at work the next morning.

'That's one way of putting it.' Yawning, Chloe sat down at her desk. 'Angela Daniels got out of bed to visit the bathroom, had a dizzy spell, fell to the floor and caused the already damaged placenta to rupture. It was only thanks to the air ambulance that we arrived at the hospital in time. I'm going to ring and see how she's doing.'

Kate gestured to the desk. 'Oliver left a message for you. He said he knew you would be worried, so he phoned St Piran first thing. Angela had a stable night and she's doing well. The baby is fine. It's all in the note.'

'Thanks.'

Tears stung Chloe's eyes and she looked away from Kate's knowing gaze. Oliver had been wonderful the previous evening. She hadn't felt at all scared when he had held her. Far from it, actually. She had felt safe and secure, so much so that she had confided to him about her mother's miscarriage. Oliver had been so understanding and supportive. And then she had fallen asleep in his arms! She couldn't believe it. Despite only having a few hours of rest, she had awoken feeling relaxed…and strangely disappointed to find herself alone. Opening her eyes to the sun-filled room, her gaze had fallen at once on the note he had left for her.

I hope you slept well. I made sure all was safe and secure before I left—and both Cyclops and Pirate were fine. Thank you for sharing part of your past with me. I'm always here for you when you feel ready to tell me the rest. You are a terrific midwife and an amazing woman. I'll see you later, babe. Call me if you need anything. Love, Oliver x

It made her smile just thinking of him. He was nothing like she had first imagined him to be when he had joined the practice. Lauren and Kate were right. There was so much more to him than the sexy surfer image. He was smart and funny, kind and thoughtful…all qualities that came naturally to him. But always there was that underlying thread of intimacy, of warmth and caring, that made her feel both nervous and giddily excited.

Remembering how he had signed the note made her think of claiming the kiss he had left her. Which made her think of kissing in general. After her lesson the previous evening, when he had shown her how magical and arousing it could be, how wonderful he tasted, how incredible he made her feel, she could kiss Oliver for ever. She felt hot and tingly just thinking about it and she couldn't wait to do it again. Funny that she had never been interested before, had never spent a second considering it, and now, thanks to a few hours and a couple of kisses with Oliver, she could think of little else.

Chloe worried that Oliver saw more than he should. He was frighteningly attuned to her, the only person who saw deeper than the surface veneer she had worn for more years than she could remember. She had a few close friends, including Kate, but it was Lauren who knew more about her than anyone. Yet even from her she kept back an awful lot. That Oliver saw the person inside both scared her witless and made her feel secure, cared for, warm.

Although Oliver was aware of her inexperience, and now knew about her mother losing the baby—and why—she was worried that if she did bring herself to confide more about the nature of her childhood, she would drive him away. He had said he wanted to know, that nothing would change how he felt, but she wasn't so sure. She was ashamed of her past, of her father and the legacy his brand of abuse had bestowed on her, and she wasn't sure she could handle the emotions that might flood out if she unlocked things she had kept hidden so deeply inside her for years.

'Oliver told me he'd sorted things out with Nick about the antenatal work.' Kate's comment drew her from her reverie. She looked up, saw her friend's brave smile, and knew the situation with Nick still hurt her. 'I think the compromise will suit everyone—and our Friday meetings should be more comfortable.'

'I hope so. Have you spoken to Nick?'

Kate averted her gaze. 'Only in passing—about work. That's an improvement, anyway.'

'Kate…'

'I know, my love. But Nick has to come round to things in his own time. He's not ready yet to consider letting Jem into his life.' She sighed, sipping her coffee. 'I know people see Nick as being aloof, and he can be, but I've know him a long time, known the losses and disappointments he has endured, the responsibilities he's shouldered. He finds it hard to address his feelings—to open himself up to more hurt and loss.'

Chloe nodded. It was true that there was much she didn't know about Nick, or his relationship with Kate. She just thought her friend deserved someone who would make her happy rather than bring her so much angst and uncertainty.

'How are things going with you and Oliver?' Kate asked, changing the subject.

Again Chloe fought a blush. 'OK.'

'You've been seeing him?'

'Yes.' Closing the file in front of her, Chloe folded her arms and leaned on the desk. 'He's been very patient, very kind. I've really enjoyed his company.'

'That's wonderful!' Kate smiled in delight, a twinkle in her eyes. 'He's a very genuine man. Not to mention an exceedingly handsome one!'

Chloe couldn't deny that, even if she did still wonder why he wanted to be with her when any number of women would be after him. She met Kate's gaze and felt warmth stain her cheeks. 'He kissed me.'

'And?'

'I liked it,' she admitted.

She had more than *liked* it. She was impatient to kiss him again. And, she realised, she was coming to more than *like* Oliver, too.

'I'm really pleased for you, Chloe. You deserve to find happiness.' Kate paused, her expression turning serious. 'If you feel something for Oliver, if he is awakening you to the things you have missed and never known before, don't be too scared to go for it. He's a good man. He'll look after you.'

'That's what Lauren said. But what if he is just passing through? What if he leaves Penhally when his contract ends and I'm nothing but a diversion?' she asked, acknowledging and voicing her fears aloud for the first time.

'I believe Oliver is far more serious about you than that. Have you asked him why he came back to Cornwall?'

Chloe shook her head. 'No. We haven't discussed that.'

He had told her all about his childhood, funny tales from medical school, snippets about his London life, but he had never said if he was back in Cornwall for good. She was scared to ask, scared to be told he would be leaving soon.

'Don't lose this chance, my love. See Oliver for the man he is. Something special, some*one* special, doesn't come around very often.' Kate paused, a sadness and depth of experience in her eyes that made Chloe believe her friend was thinking about Nick. 'Ask yourself what you want most, how you feel when you are with him—and how you would feel if he *did* leave and you had never taken that risk.'

The phone rang then, announcing that her first patient had arrived, bringing an end to her conversation with her friend.

Kate gathered up her things. 'I'm off on my home visits. If I have time, I'll call in at the Trevellyans' farm. Fran was sounding down last time we spoke and I'd like to check up on her. My first visit is to Susan Fiddick.'

'I thought she went to the hospital yesterday.'

'She did…and the scan shows the baby is still breech. But she insisted on coming home, ignoring St Piran's advice for the Caesarean.' Kate looked concerned. 'I'm hoping to talk her round—and Nick said he would speak to her as well.'

Chloe offered a sympathetic smile. However natural they tried to keep the whole pregnancy and birthing process, some-times it wasn't easy matching the woman's wishes with the safest care. Not when nature intervened and things didn't go according to plan.

'Good luck. I hope everything works out.'

'Thanks.' Kate paused on her way to the door. 'I hope things work out for you, too. With Oliver. Think about what I said, my love.'

And think she did. Throughout a morning busy with appointments at the surgery, followed by an afternoon of home visits around the district, Oliver was never far from her mind. When she arrived back in Penhally, she was running late, with time only to sort out her paperwork and grab a quick snack before her evening duty at the well-woman clinic. Things were winding down in the surgery when she went in, but Sue was behind the reception desk and waved her across.

'Everything all right?' Chloe asked with a smile.

'It's been manic.' Looking stressed, Sue grimaced. 'Kate is in St Piran. She was called back out a couple of hours ago when Susan Fiddick went into labour. *Now* she's finally agreed to intervention.'

Chloe shook her head. Poor Kate. And poor Susan. 'What about Jem?'

'He's staying over with a school friend.' Sue shuffled her messages. 'Here we go. These are for you. And Oliver has asked you to see him before you head off for the clinic. He's finished his patient list.'

'OK.'

Chloe's stomach filled with butterflies and her heart skittered. Why did Oliver want to see her? Was it about work…or something else? Feeling breathless, she hurried up the stairs to drop off her things and put her patient files away, then headed back down to the consulting rooms. Oliver's door stood ajar and she paused a moment watching him, noting the uncharacteristic frown on his face as he studied some papers.

She tapped on the door. Their gazes met and she was surprised at the serious expression in those devilish brown eyes. 'You wanted to see me?'

'Chloe, hi.' The smoky tones of Oliver's voice did curious things to her insides.

'Is there a problem?'

'Come in a minute.' He rose to his feet and crossed to meet her, closing the door before dropping a brief kiss on her lips. 'Take a seat.'

He perched on the edge of the desk near her and a very different fluttering, this time of unease, knotted her stomach. 'What's wrong?'

'It's about the Morrisons,' he told her.

'Baby Timmy?' She rubbed suddenly damp palms on her trousers. 'Oliver?'

A ragged sigh escaped. 'The results have come back from the heel-prick tests.'

'Already? And?'

'Chloe...the test for cystic fibrosis is positive.'

Her fingers clenched around the arms of the chair, her knuckles white as she battled away the unprofessional sting of tears. She knew she became too involved with her mums and their babies. She couldn't help it. Her job meant the world to her. Beth and Jason had tried so long for their baby and had suffered two miscarriages before little Timmy had come along this summer. There had been nothing in their history to suggest cystic fibrosis was a worry, no family incidence. But they must both be carriers and the one in four chance had hit them.

'Chloe?'

'Have you told them?' Somehow she forced the words out, pushing the image of Timmy from her mind.

'Not yet. And not without you. I didn't want you finding out alone, seeing the report left on your desk.' He paused, reaching out to take one of her hands in his. 'Maybe you would like it if we break the news to them together?'

His thoughtfulness touched her and she quelled a fresh threat of tears, unconsciously curling her fingers with his. 'Yes. Thank you. The test isn't conclusive,' she added, grasping at straws.

'No. There will be much to discuss with Beth and Jason, and further investigations to authenticate the results with a DNA test for the delta F508 gene. If CF *is* confirmed, we can bring Lauren in as soon as possible to help with physiotherapy needs.'

'Yes.' Chloe nodded, scarcely able to take it in.

'You know early diagnosis means much more successful treatment and longer life expectancy. We start treatment and physio before there is lung damage, and refer to a specialist CF centre.'

Knowing she wasn't going to hold on much longer, she withdrew her hand from his and rose unsteadily to her feet, unable to meet his all-seeing gaze. 'Thanks for the information. Let me know when to be available to see the Morrisons.'

She turned and walked to the door, one hand pressed to her lips to hold in the sob that fought to escape. Her free hand fumbled with the doorhandle. Just when she managed to open it, desperate to be alone, she felt Oliver behind her, his hand reaching past her to hold the door closed and then lock it. She froze.

'Chloe…'

The gentleness in that husky voice threatened to undo her. 'I need to go.'

'No. Come here, babe.'

Hands settled on her shoulders and turned her to face him. Her eyes widened in confusion, tears shimmering on her lashes, and she tried to blink them back, but a couple escaped, dropping onto her cheeks. He cupped her face, his thumbs brushing the moisture away. A shiver ran through her, and she felt uncertain when he drew her closer, tucking her head against his chest with one hand, his other arm curling around her.

'Oliver?' She held herself stiffly in his embrace.

'You're upset. Take a few moments. Let me cuddle you.'

Being held like this should have spooked her—would have done had it been any man but Oliver. Wrapped in his embrace she felt both anxious yet safe. Beneath her cheek she could feel the steady, calming beat of his heart. To her surprise, she began to relax, allowing her hands to rest at his waist, her fingers feeling the play of muscle beneath firm flesh through the thin fabric of his shirt. Another few moments and instinct had her leaning into him, her arms sliding around him, while his free hand stroked her back, and his husky, whispered words soothed her. She had no idea how long they stayed that way, but gradually she felt calmer, stronger.

Although he relaxed his hold, Oliver didn't let her go, but he pulled back far enough to look down and meet her gaze.

Embarrassed, Chloe bit her lip. 'I'm sorry.'

'Never apologise for caring.'

'I'm a professional, I—'

'You are also human. And you're so good at your job because of how you feel about the mums and their babies.' Sincerity and understanding shone in his brown eyes. 'It's been a difficult couple of days. This news about Timmy, on top of the emergency with Angela, was bound to affect you. The day it doesn't is the day any of us should stop doing this job.'

Aware he was still holding her close, that her body was responding in unfamiliar ways, Chloe found the strength to place some much-needed distance between them. His nearness addled her senses and turned her brain to mush. She more than liked him, was coming to trust him, but she still felt nervous of all the new and unknown sensations assailing her.

'I'm OK now.'

Oliver frowned, unconvinced, but he allowed her to retreat. 'Are you sure?'

'Yes. Thanks.' She managed a smile, grateful for his support. 'I have to get ready for the well-woman clinic.'

Something she didn't recognise crossed his expression as he looked down at her. 'All right. I'll talk to you later, babe,' he promised, tucking a stray wisp of hair behind her ear, his fingers lingering for a moment before he dropped a firmer kiss on her mouth, then stepped back.

Chloe let herself out of the room, jogging up the stairs to her own office where she sank into her chair, one fist pressed against her chest. Why did she feel so strange? Yes, she was upset about the news of Timmy Morrison's positive test, but Oliver had been empathetic, helping her over the initial shock, and he had managed to ground her again. He had been right— she would have hated to find the report on her desk, cold, with no warning. Sharing it with him, knowing he cared too, had made it easier. What she found less easy to understand were the raging emotions she felt when she was with him, the way her body reacted when he touched her.

Somehow she got through the evening, grateful that the clinic was busy. Oliver had been right, it had been a hell of a week. He had understood her, but she knew she took things too personally with her mums and babies. She couldn't help it. She became so involved in them and their lives, but it often cost her emotionally. Unfortunately her duty at the clinic meant she couldn't see Oliver, or Lauren, that evening. She would have liked to have talked to someone, she reflected as she walked home along the harbour front to her cosy cottage in Fisherman's Row.

She liked her home. It was the first place she'd been able to call her own. The first place where she felt safe and settled. After greeting Pirate and Cyclops, she fed them, then went upstairs to shower, washing the stresses of the day away before changing into a cool top and shorts. Padding back down to the kitchen, she made herself a sandwich, then sat in the living room with the patio doors open and tried to relax.

She went to bed early, but felt restless and edgy, as well as uncomfortably warm. Her window was open, but there was scant breeze off the harbour to ease the sultry night air. When the phone rang, startling her, she picked up the receiver, hoping none of her mums-to-be had a problem.

'Hello. Chloe MacKinnon.'

'Hi, babe.'

The throaty voice sent a prickle along her spine. 'O-Oliver! Is something wrong?' She propped herself up against the pillows, frowning with confusion.

'I wanted to see how you were feeling,' he explained. 'Did I wake you?'

'No, it's too hot to sleep. I can't stop thinking about little Timmy,' she admitted after a pause, something about the dark and the connection she felt with Oliver making it easier to admit her worries.

'I know. Sometimes things are horribly unfair.' She could tell by his voice that he genuinely cared. 'We'll find a time between our appointments tomorrow when we're both free and we'll talk to Beth and Jason together.'

'Thank you.'

They discussed the Morrisons a while longer, then moved away from work, talking comfortably about anything and everything. Chloe snuggled down, relaxing, a smile on her face as Oliver's husky voice and rumbly laugh sounded in her ear.

'I missed seeing you tonight,' he told her softly some time later.

Biting her lip, Chloe gripped the receiver tighter, affected by the warm intimacy of his voice, longing for him knotting her stomach. 'Me, too.'

'Yeah?' She heard the smile in his voice, thought she also

heard the faint rustle of a sheet. Was he in bed, too? The image made her even hotter. 'We'll do something nice together at the weekend.'

'I'd like that,' she agreed, all too quickly, the prospect of spending time with him bringing a rush of excited anticipation.

'Do you think you can sleep now?'

She *did* feel languorous and at ease. Just talking with him had done that for her. It had been what she had needed without even knowing it. But Oliver had. 'Yes, I think so. Thank you for ringing.'

'No problem. I've enjoyed it,' he assured her.

'Me, too.' So much so she didn't want it to end. 'Goodnight, Oliver.'

'Goodnight, babe. Sweet dreams. I'll see you in the morning.'

When the click sounded in her ear, indicating that Oliver had hung up, she felt stupidly alone, but also had a warm, fuzzy, fluttering inside her tummy.

She had only known him a few weeks, but she was discovering how much she had misjudged him at the beginning. He wasn't the fast-living playboy gossip had suggested, but an instinctive, fantastic doctor, and a man who treated her with infinite patience, caring and sensitivity. She had never once felt threatened, pressured or unsafe. And as for his kisses… Oh, my! Oliver made her feel things she had never felt before, stirred things inside her that she wasn't sure how to handle. She just knew she didn't want them to stop.

CHAPTER SIX

'I'M SORRY. I'd forgotten about today.' As Chloe glanced up, Oliver saw regret in her eyes. 'We don't have to stay long, but I promised Eloise I'd come by.'

'Don't worry about it, babe. We've had a great weekend…and I have plans for later,' he added, his voice dropping as he murmured in her ear, close enough to feel her quiver in response.

Dressed in denim shorts and a loose cotton shirt knotted at the waist, which left her midriff bare, Chloe looked good enough to eat. His hunger for her only increased with every passing day. Resting one hand at the small of her back, enjoying the feel of her super-soft skin under his palm, Oliver guided her along the beach towards the spot where the informal barbecue party was well under way.

'Remind me again what we're celebrating.'

Chloe smiled up at him. 'Eloise Hayden and Lachlan D'Ancey's engagement.'

'He's the local police chief?' Oliver asked, his gaze scanning the gathering for people he knew.

'He lives in Penhally but he's based at the station in Wadebridge,' Chloe explained. 'He met Eloise, an Australian forensic pathologist, when she came over last month to give a second opinion on a surfer's death.'

Oliver nodded. 'I heard the talk, but I've never met Lachlan or Eloise.'

'They are really nice. There's Eloise, talking to Kate. Shall we say hello?'

'Sure.'

As Chloe led the way, he reflected on the last couple of days. Friday had been difficult, meeting the Morrisons and breaking the news about Timmy's results. But Beth and Jason had been strong, drawing on the support and encouragement Chloe had given them. He knew better than anyone how the news had affected Chloe, and he was so proud of the care and compassion she offered to her patients. If the next round of tests confirmed that Timmy did have cystic fibrosis, he knew that the family would have first-class support from Chloe, Lauren and himself, as well as whatever specialist advice could be offered to them.

After the success of his Thursday night phone call, speaking to each other last thing before they went to sleep had become a habit. Even if he had only just parted from her, they still talked for a few moments on the phone. It was special…and increased even more his growing need to be with her, to not have to leave her at all.

On Saturday, after morning appointments, he and Chloe had gone for a ride on their motorbikes, then had spent the evening cuddled up at her cottage, watching a DVD, talking, drinking wine and doing a lot of kissing. They were winding up the intimacy and the passion, with deeper, hotter kisses and some tantalising, teasing touches. He made sure he left her wanting more, but it also drove him insane with his own desire for her. Faced with Chloe's increasing confidence and eagerness, it was becoming ever more difficult to keep a tight rein on his control. But he wanted her to be ready, to ask for what she wanted, to need him as much as he needed her.

He had never been that into kissing before. It was too

intimate somehow, and past relationships had been more about instant gratification—on both sides. The full joy of devoting time to kissing, without rush and pressure, had passed him by. Until now. He could kiss Chloe for hours, days…for ever. Knowing he had to take things slowly with her brought everything back to basics, to endless hours of foreplay and hot, sexy, incredibly intimate and satisfying kisses. It was like nothing he had ever known before. There was no demand to perform, no haste for fulfilment. The drawn-out loving, leading to the blossoming of Chloe's sensuality, was reward in itself. For now. If he felt this charged from kissing her, he'd probably combust when he finally made love to her.

Plans for today had changed when Chloe had remembered the beach barbecue. Oliver was just content to be with her, whatever the circumstances. It was a major advance that she was unconcerned at them being seen in public as a couple. He cared about her and he wanted people to know that. In staking his claim, he was taking a risk, putting himself on the line, but, as he discovered more every day, Chloe was worth it.

After being introduced to Eloise and talking with her, Kate and Chloe for a few minutes, Oliver accepted Eloise's invitation to head to the barbecue buffet table and fetch some refreshments for himself and Chloe.

'I'll catch up with you in a few minutes,' he promised, leaving her with her friends.

Chloe watched Oliver saunter with deceptive lazy grace across the sand towards the food table where Lachlan was in charge of the barbecue. Oliver looked equally stunning in the faded jeans and body-hugging T-shirt he wore today as he did in the smart clothes he wore for work. She turned back to find Kate and Eloise watching her, knowing smiles on their faces. Chloe fought a blush.

'Any improvements in the situation with Nick?' Eloise

asked, and, although thankful to have escaped questions about Oliver, Chloe felt sorry for Kate. Eloise was the only other person who knew about Jem's real father.

'Things have settled down a little at work.' Kate managed a smile, her gaze straying to Jem, who was playing beach cricket with some friends. 'But Nick isn't ready to face the reality that Jem is his son. I don't know if he ever will be.'

Chloe looked around the assembled group. 'Is Nick not here?'

'No.' Kate's disappointment was obvious. 'He's gone to France for the weekend with the twinning committee. They have meetings in Normandy.'

They chatted for a few moments, then other people claimed Eloise's attention. Kate went to talk with Lucy and Ben, smiling as she cuddled their baby daughter, Annabel, whom she had delivered in difficult circumstances last Christmas. Chloe wished her friend could be as content in all aspects of her life. Turning away, she looked for Oliver, seeing he was still at the food table, talking with Lachlan, Dragan and Melinda. As she headed in that direction, she bumped into Eve Dwyer.

'Hello, Chloe, good to see you.'

'And you, Eve. How are things?' she asked the older woman.

'I'm fine. A bit tired of the commute to Newquay,' she admitted. 'I'll be so glad when a practice nurse vacancy comes up here in Penhally.' Eve paused a moment, glancing around to check they were not being overheard. 'Is the rumour about Rachel Kenner and Gary Lovelace true?'

Frowning, Chloe nodded. 'I'm afraid so. Poor Rachel. Gary treated her terribly.'

'How is she coping?' Eve asked, ever the compassionate nurse.

'She was very frightened, especially about facing her

father,' Chloe admitted. 'But you know how lovely Reverend Kenner is, and how much he cares for Rachel.'

Eve nodded, looking distracted. 'So he's supporting her?'

'Very much so. I'm seeing her regularly and she's determined to keep the baby while still following her dream to be a teacher,' she told her, explaining about the aunt and uncle in Plymouth.

'That's good.'

Chloe caught an edge in Eve's tone and realised the other woman looked pale and strained. 'Eve, are you all right?'

'I'm fine.' Her gaze slid away and she redirected the conversation. 'That family. Tassie is the only one with any goodness in her.'

'She's lucky to have your care and support,' Chloe praised, admiring of all Eve was trying to do for the troubled young girl.

'Tassie's not had much of a start in life. But even at ten she plans to be different from the rest of them, to use her brains to make a good life for herself. I want to help her.'

Eve still looked troubled and again Chloe voiced her concern. 'Are you sure you're OK?'

'Don't worry, Chloe. Just a shadow from the past,' the older woman murmured cryptically.

Before Chloe could question her further, Oliver arrived at her side, handing her a plate of food and a drink. 'Here we go, babe.'

'Thanks.' Chloe introduced him to Eve. The other woman seemed eager to leave, so Chloe had to let the subject drop. 'That was strange.'

Distracted, Oliver took a bite of his fish. 'Hmm?'

'Nothing,' Chloe murmured, watching Eve walk away, her shoulders hunched as if she carried the weight of the world on them.

Her worry about Eve dissipated as she and Oliver talked while enjoying their food. Afterwards, they mingled for a short time, and Chloe was supremely conscious of Oliver beside her, touching her, one hand at the hollow of her back, warm against her bare skin. The pad of his thumb dipped under the waistband of her shorts and traced tiny circles at the base of her spine…devastating, enticing, strength-sapping touches. So simple, yet so seductive. Her legs felt shaky and there was a heavy knot in her stomach. All she could think about was how wonderful the weekend had been, how amazing it was to kiss him, how much she wanted to be alone with him again, how special it had become that his voice on the phone was the last thing she had heard the last three nights before she had fallen asleep.

'Ready to leave, babe?'

His voice was a husky whisper in her ear, his warm breath fanning her skin, sending tingles of awareness through her whole body. She met his sinful dark gaze, feeling hotter than ever, and nodded. 'Yes.'

He bestowed on her the kind of smile that always made her breathless, then took her hand, linking their fingers. After they had said their goodbyes, he led her back along the harbour front to his car and before long they were heading out of town.

'Why are we here?' she asked a while later as Oliver pulled into the parking area at a watersports centre a short way along the coast from Penhally.

'Knowing how you love motorbikes, I have an adventure planned.'

'What kind of adventure?' Anxiety gnawed in the pit of her stomach.

He slanted her a glance, dark eyes sparkling with mischief. 'I'm taking you jet-skiing.'

Chloe forced herself to climb out of the car. Part of her wanted to experience the thrill of riding a jet-ski, but she couldn't get beyond the fear that gripped her. She didn't want her past to keep impinging on the rest of her life. In the time she had known Oliver she had faced many of her demons but…

Her footsteps slowed, her heart thudded under her ribs. What was she going to do? How could she tell Oliver?

It took a few seconds before Oliver realised that Chloe was no longer walking with him towards the beachfront office where they would pick up the two-seater jet-ski he had hired. If Chloe enjoyed their outing, he planned to buy her a present—a single-person machine like his so they could go out on the water together. He turned round, noting the paleness of her face, the shadow of fear in her wary green eyes. Hell. He'd done something wrong. Walking back, he took both her hands in his.

'What's happened?' He searched her gaze, could feel her shaking. 'Talk to me, babe. Tell me whatever it is you're feeling.'

'I—I'm scared. Of the water. I nearly drowned once.'

'Damn, I'm sorry.' Oliver wanted to kick himself. Instead, he wrapped her in a gentle hug. 'I had no idea.' He pulled back enough to look into her eyes, seeing the uncertainty in their green depths. 'I didn't mean to upset you.'

'You haven't. It's not you. It's *him.*'

Confused, he lightly rubbed his hands up and down her bare arms. 'Him?' he queried, trying to make sense of what she was saying.

'My father.'

When she exhaled a ragged breath, he led her off the path towards a low wall. Sitting next to her, he slipped an arm around her, his free hand holding one of hers. 'Tell me.'

'I was about seven. I never understood why he went into rages, what put sudden ideas in his head, but this day he marched me down to the rocks.' Her fingers tightened on his and Oliver cuddled her closer, feeling icy cold despite the heat of the day. 'I'd never swum. My mother was always scared and kept me away from the water, and though I loved the beach, I suppose her fear rubbed off on me. Something set my father off, and he said I could learn to swim or drown.' Chloe's voice wavered. 'He picked me up and tossed me in. I did nearly drown. A couple of nearby fishermen pulled me out. They threatened to tell the police but my father insisted it had been an accident and persuaded them to keep quiet.'

Horrified, he didn't know what to say. 'God, Chloe.'

This was another confidence, another sign of her coming to trust him. But it was also another piece in the jigsaw that her father was responsible for the horrors of her childhood. He hated it that he had made her face something upsetting when all he had wanted was for her to have fun this weekend.

'I'll cancel the booking. We'll go somewhere else,' he reassured her, startled when she pushed against him, her head shaking vigorously.

'No!'

'Chloe?'

She turned to face him, grasping his hand. 'I don't want to let him win, Oliver. I don't want to be afraid of things because of him for the rest of my life. You've opened my eyes to so much recently. You must think I'm really stupid,' she finished on a whisper, ducking her head.

'That's the very last thing I think of you.' His heart swelled with emotion. He couldn't bear to imagine all she had been through, couldn't bear to consider what else her father had done to her, what more he still had to learn about her childhood. Holding her close, he stroked her hair. 'I think you're amazing. And I'm so proud of you. Whatever you want to do, I'm here to help. Whenever you're ready to talk, I'm here to listen.'

She raised her head, disbelief and hope warring in her eyes, a shaky smile hovering at her mouth, making him want to kiss her senseless. 'Oliver?'

'Yes, babe?' He cleared his throat, his voice sounding raw to his own ears.

'Take me jet-skiing.'

* * *

She had to be crazy. Chloe choked down a nervous laugh. Here she was in a wetsuit and impact buoyancy vest about to face one of her nightmares. She was frightened. But she trusted Oliver—and what she had told him was true. She didn't want to spend the rest of her life being afraid, didn't want what Lauren had said to be true…that her father was still ruling her life from the grave. Oliver had changed her. He gave her strength and courage. She *was* scared, had no idea where all this might lead, but she was tired of living in the shadows.

'Chloe, look at me.' He cupped her face, raising her gaze to his. 'You can change your mind at any time.'

Her chest was tight and she felt sick, but she shook her head. 'No.'

'We're going *on* the water, not *in* it. There is no way on this earth that I would let anything bad happen to you.'

'I know.' She believed it, believed the earnest sincerity in his dark eyes as they looked deeply into her own.

'Trust me.'

Feeling this was now about far more than a ride on jet-ski, she tentatively placed her hand in his, immediately feeling enveloped by his gentle strength. Oliver sat her in front of him, his arms reaching round her to the controls, cocooning her in his protective embrace.

'OK?'

She nodded, trying to bank down her fear of the water, relaxing a little as he nuzzled her, pressing a kiss to the sensitive hollow below her ear. They started slowly, easing out from the shore, the water calm and smooth along this stretch of coast, for which she was heartily thankful. It didn't take her long to get used to the unfamiliar motion and, to her surprise, she began to enjoy it, feeling incredibly safe with Oliver watching over her. After a while he drew to a halt and they drifted for a few moments, the engine idling as they looked back towards the spectacular Cornish coastline.

'All right, babe?'

Nodding, she glanced round to smile at him. 'I'm fine. Thank you.'

'Thank *you*—for trusting me.' Before she could say anything, his mouth met hers in a brief but stirring kiss. 'Ready to move on?'

Sensing that there was more than one meaning to his words, Chloe's insides fluttered in nervous excitement. 'Yes,' she told him shyly, earning herself the kind of dimpled smile that would have weakened her knees had she not already been sitting down.

'Faster?'

'Faster,' she agreed, feeling warm and giddy with happiness at his carefree laugh and the glowing approval in his eyes.

They had a fun time. It was exhilarating, riding with Oliver, the spray hitting their faces. And always she felt safe, never sensing he was taking risks or trying to play the macho show-off. When they finally arrived back at the shore, Oliver slipped off, holding her steady and seeing her gently onto dry land. Then she did something she had never done in her life. She spontaneously hugged him, carried along by pure joy and emotion, the freedom from a part of her past that had held her back for so long. Could she now move on and let go of the other chains that bound her?

She couldn't think about that now because Oliver's arms closed around her, holding her close, making her all too aware of him, the strength of his athletic body pressed against her, the heady masculine scent of him. Her smile faded at the look in his eyes…intense, fiery hunger. Then his head lowered, his mouth taking hers, and she surrendered to the magic of his kiss.

'I hear you're something of a hero.'

Oliver's eyes opened at Chloe's words and he smiled tiredly. 'Hardly.'

He'd been more relieved than ever to leave work, dash to the flat for a quick shower and change of clothes, and then meet up with Chloe to enjoy a quiet meal at her cottage before relaxing on the sofa. Taking her hand, he shifted his position and drew her towards him, encouraging her to sit on his lap facing him, her legs straddling his. Grateful to hold her close, he breathed in the familiar scent of sunshine and fresh, fruity apples, feeling settled and grounded with her in his arms. Meeting her gaze, he saw the concern in her green eyes as she brushed a wayward fall of hair back from his face before resting her hands on his shoulders. He was encouraged that she was so comfortable with the new intimacy that had continued to build after their passionate kiss following their jet ski outing several days ago.

'I came back from house calls—one of which was to Avril Harvey, by the way, and she and her daughter are doing fine—to hear you'd had a run-in with Nick,' she prompted.

'That's good news about the Harveys.' His smile faded as he answered the other part of her comment. 'As for Nick, he didn't want me going out to see Henry Ryall, said we'd wasted enough time on the man, that there was nothing wrong with him.'

Chloe frowned. 'That doesn't sound like Nick. He can be difficult, but he puts patients first.'

'I know.' Oliver's frown mirrored Chloe's. Nick was still stressed and edgy. Clearly the problem with Kate had not been resolved. 'Anyway, he's been out to Henry's farm more than once in the last month, so have Dragan and Adam. No one found anything wrong with him. They'd all done everything by the book, there was no reason to believe that Henry was sick,' he admitted, recalling Nick's arguments. 'The consensus of opinion was that Henry was sad and lonely having recently lost his wife…'

'But?' Chloe raised an eyebrow, as if knowing that wouldn't be good enough for him.

'I don't like writing people off too soon. And I can't explain it, but I had a hunch, one I didn't want to ignore. Nick told me to go and waste my time if I wanted to.'

'You were right, though, and it wasn't a waste of time.'

Sighing, Oliver ran his hands down her back to her delectable rear end, pulling her even closer. 'It was a complete fluke that I happened to be there at that precise moment.'

'Having weak tea and stale biscuits,' Chloe teased, making him smile. He'd discovered Henry's infamous idea of 'refreshments' for himself.

'I'd checked Henry's notes, spoken with Dragan, Adam and Nick. Henry had reported banging his head twice in the same place in the last weeks, but they'd all done the right examinations and checks and could find nothing wrong with him,' he explained, the fingers of one hand finding the gap between the waistband of her jeans and the bottom of her shirt, enjoying the feel of satiny skin. 'Henry couldn't give a clear picture of what was wrong, just that things weren't right, that he felt foggy and was still having headaches. He seemed fine when I first got there and I thought maybe Nick was right and I *was* wasting my time.'

'But you weren't?'

'No. I did the same examinations, checked the reaction of his pupils, tested if he could balance on one leg, walk in a straight line, could touch the end of his nose with one finger with his eyes shut…all the usual things. I monitored his blood pressure and gave him a thorough health check. There was no sign of anything amiss.'

Looking puzzled, Chloe sat back and watched him. 'So what happened?'

'We were talking, I was getting ready to leave, and suddenly Henry's mouth was moving but no sound was coming out.' He shook his head, still unable to believe the timing of it, wondering what would have happened had Henry been alone and unable to raise help. 'One moment he was speaking normally, the next he was looking bemused and frightened, unable to speak.'

'Wow.' Chloe's eyes widened in amazement.

Smiling, Oliver tucked a strand of hair that had escaped her braid back behind her ear. 'It was bizarre. But something I'd seen before. I took Henry straight to hospital, they did a CT scan and discovered a small bleed in his brain. He's having an operation to repair it and he should make a good recovery.'

'How could that happen?'

'Sometimes with a head injury you can have this slow, tiny bleed that causes no outward symptoms for a time. It didn't help that Henry hit his head twice in the same place in rapid succession. No one could have known. There was nothing to alert Dragan, Adam or Nick, no reason for them to send Henry for further tests. As I said, it was pure chance I happened to be there.'

Chloe dropped a kiss on his mouth. 'I'm glad you were. Lucky Henry. And I hope Nick was apologetic.'

'He was.' Oliver couldn't resist giving her another kiss before he continued. 'To be fair, he waited on at the surgery for me to get back from St Piran to talk about it. That's why I was late.'

'I'm just glad Henry is going to be all right.'

'Me, too.' He raised his free hand to cup her face. 'And I'm glad to be here with you now.' Brushing the pad of his thumb along the fullness of her lower lip, he held her gaze. 'I desperately want to kiss you.'

Creamy cheeks turned rosy as she flushed and her voice was breathy. 'Do you?'

'Oh, yeah!'

'OK.' She smiled, sinking against him. Her mouth was honey sweet, so eager and welcoming that he was instantly lost, his control on the ragged edge.

* * *

Chloe couldn't hold back a whimper of needy excitement as she lost herself in the taste and feel and scent of Oliver. They had spent every moment they could together since the jet-ski outing on Sunday, and she was feeling closer to him than ever. As well as increasingly frustrated when he kept calling a halt to their ever more passionate kisses before she wanted to stop. She was impatient for more…she just wasn't sure what *more* was, or how to persuade Oliver she was ready. He was so determined to take things slowly. She was also unsure what all this meant to him. His care seemed genuine but, as she had mentioned to Kate, was she just a diversion for Oliver? Did he plan to stay in Penhally Bay?

Reluctantly, she pulled back from the kiss, seeing his eyes darken with a desire that matched her own. One of his hands rested on her back under her shirt, sending heat permeating throughout her body. She wanted his hand to move. Wanted to touch him, too. Licking her lips, noting the flare of response in his eyes as he watched her, she shifted even closer, bringing their bodies more intimately into contact. Her own eyes widened as she felt the undeniable evidence of his arousal. Nervous, not sure how far she wanted to take this, she hesitated.

'Chloe?' Oliver's voice was rough and she was excited that she could affect him like this.

'About my lessons.'

A smile dimpled his cheek but the hungry look in his eyes didn't fade. Her pulse skittered as his fingers began a gentle caress up and down her spine. 'You're not enjoying them?'

'You have to know I am,' she protested, unable to prevent herself pouting at him.

A chuckle rumbled from his chest. 'But?'

'I'm ready to move on to a more advanced level.'

'I see.' The fingers on her back stilled for a moment. 'And what do you expect the next steps to be?'

Faced with the intensity of his gaze and the smoky rough-ness of his voice, some of her nerve deserted her. 'Um…I don't know. I just feel…'

'Tell me what you feel, babe,' he encouraged when she paused, distracting her by nibbling along her jaw.

'When you kiss me and touch me, I feel all tingly and achy and heavy.' Long, thick lashes lifted and she couldn't look away from the heat in his dark gaze. She swallowed, search-ing for the right words to explain. 'I don't want you to stop as soon as you do. I need you to touch me in other places…and I want to touch you, too.'

She was surprised and pleased when Oliver drew in a ragged breath. 'Are you sure?'

'Yes.'

Sinking her fingers into the thickness of his hair, she kissed him with eager enthusiasm, unable to get enough of him. When he sucked on her tongue, drawing her into the hot sweetness of his mouth, it was so erotic and inflaming that she feared she would explode, need tightening almost painfully inside her. Pulling back a few inches, she looked down, her fingers shaking as she began to inch up the fabric of his T-shirt, exposing a flat stomach with a narrow trail of dark hair disap-pearing beneath the waistband of his jeans. She pushed the fabric higher, revealing a toned abdomen and broad chest…olive-hued skin, supple flesh and hard muscle. Helping her, he pulled the T-shirt over his head and for a moment she just studied him, heat prickling along every nerve ending. He was beautiful. There was no other word to describe the mas-culine perfection of him. Hesitating, she spotted the dark ring encircling the bicep of his left arm.

'You have a tattoo.' Surprised, she investigated the narrow barbed band usually hidden by his clothes.

'I have two,' he told her.

Her gaze met his, seeing the amused mischief in his dark brown eyes. 'Where's the other one?'

'You can look for it another time.'

Disappointed, she frowned at him. 'Why not now?'

'Because my control is finite,' he warned her with a wry smile. 'And if I'm going to survive this next lesson, no way are you going anywhere near my other tattoo.'

Her heart skittered, her mind racing as she wondered just where it was. 'Oliver…'

'No, babe. Not now.' He shifted as if uncomfortable, again making her aware of his arousal. 'Today we both keep above the waist.'

Capturing her wrists, his gaze holding hers, he slowly brought her hands to his chest. She closed her eyes, savouring her first feel of him, warm and firm, his heartbeat under her palm as rapid as her own. Her lack of expertise didn't appear to bother him and he deftly tutored her, guiding her natural responses, showing her how he liked her to touch him. Soaking up every new experience, each new texture, she brushed her fingertips over the brown orbs of his nipples, shocked at his reaction, his stifled groan, the way his body tightened.

'That feels good,' he told her huskily, allowing her to explore him at will but stopping her if she tried to dip below his waist. 'May I touch you, too?'

Her whole body quivered with nervous anticipation. Unable to find her voice, she nodded, her breath catching, her heart racing as Oliver slowly but surely undid the buttons of her shirt one by one. The backs of his fingers brushed against her skin, setting off little fires of sensation. Shaking, she bit her lip as he peeled the shirt away, sliding it down her arms, his breath catching as he took in the sight of her full breasts encased in a green lacy bra. She enjoyed wearing nice underwear. Like growing her hair long, it was a throwback to her youth and her father's control, a way of thumbing her nose at him, refusing to let him dominate everything in her life. The clasp at her back parted with a deft flick of Oliver's fingers and a mix of embarrassment, fear and excitement churned inside her as he slowly drew the straps down her arms, baring her to his view.

'You're perfect, Chloe,' he praised, his voice raw.

As his fingertips skimmed her ribs, his tanned skin looked exotic against the creamy paleness of her own. He leaned in to kiss her, lingering a while before his lips grazed away from her mouth to trail down her throat. His hands rested on her sides, while her own grasped his shoulders as she trembled, on the brink of something she didn't understand, yearning for his touch, yet scared, too.

'Oliver?'

'Slow and easy, babe,' he whispered, his voice seductive, low and husky, his breath warm against her skin as he nibbled round her neck. She started as his tongue tip tickled across the web of faded scars that fanned down to her shoulder. 'Did your father do this?'

Too lost in the moment to care what else she was revealing, she curled into his touch. 'He hit me and I fell through a glass door,' she whispered, feeling the sudden tension in Oliver's body, aware of his simmering anger on her behalf before he took a steadying breath and gentled again.

He raised his head to meet her gaze. 'Chloe…'

'Let's not talk about it now.' She didn't want to spoil this incredible moment with thoughts of her father.

After a pause, Oliver nodded, but his reluctance was clear and she knew they would have to talk at some point. Later. Much later if she had her way. She sighed as his fingers began to whisper over her skin, feather-light touches that teased and tingled and aroused.

'Your skin is impossibly soft, so warm and silky and smooth,' he told her, his voice dropping to a husky murmur. 'I love touching you.'

When his thumbs brushed the undersides of her plump, firm breasts, Chloe thought she would never breathe again. Then his hands covered her flesh fully for the first time and she was sure she had died and gone to heaven. She bit back a cry, her fingers tensing on his shoulders as she instinctively arched to his touch.

'Any time you say stop, Chloe, I'll stop.'

His murmured promise registered through the hazy fog of pleasure enveloping her, but she didn't want him to stop. Not yet. Not when this felt so fantastic. She closed her eyes, unable to focus on anything but the caress of his hands as he shaped her, his questing fingertips exploring nipples that had peaked to hard, sensitive crests. A moan escaped. She had never known anything like this. She couldn't believe the way her body was reacting, the way her breasts felt fuller and heavier, every sensation spearing deep inside her. And when Oliver touched her with his lips, lightly lapping his warm tongue around and over one nipple before he gently suckled it inside his mouth, she jolted, her body writhing in his arms.

It was so overwhelming, so new and scary and wonderful, that she pulled back. 'Stop.' Her voice was thready, mixed with confusion and doubt, yearning and desire.

Oliver immediately withdrew, and at once she regretted that the word had been pulled from her so unexpectedly. She hadn't meant it. Not really. Now she missed his touch. Surprising them both, she wrapped her arms around him, relishing the closeness, the feel of her breasts pressed against his bare chest. His hands stroked her back and she buried her face against his neck, breathing in his masculine scent, unconsciously rubbing herself against him.

'Chloe.'

She ignored the warning in his rough voice. This felt so good. The ache she had told him about had intensified between

er legs and she instinctively pressed herself against his
ardness. Oliver groaned and put some distance between them.

'Enough now, babe.' He sounded tense, and she raised her
ead to look at him, seeing colour flush across his cheekbones,
train etched on his handsome features.

'Did I do something wrong?'

'Hell, no. But this is getting out of hand. It's too soon for
ou…and my control is at breaking point.'

Intrigued, she smiled at him. 'Really?'

'You're wicked!'

That seemed not to be an entirely bad thing as he was
aughing. However, he gently but firmly eased her away from
im, drawing her shirt back up her arms, unsteady fingers re-
astening her buttons before he pulled his own T-shirt back over
is head. All too soon, he was lifting her off his lap and rising
o his feet.

'I think it's time I said goodnight.'

Chloe heard the regret in his voice, felt her own sense of
inking disappointment, but at the same time she knew he was
ight. She wasn't yet ready to ask him to stay. There were
hings she had to come to terms with inside herself before she
vas free to move on, and she knew she had to open her past to
Oliver and confide in him before she took the irrevocable step
of letting him take her to bed.

Her body alive and buzzing, she walked him to the door,
njoying a last, lingering, passionate kiss before he left.
Sighing, Chloe locked the door and leaned back against it,
unable to comprehend how her life had changed so drastically
n the few short weeks since she had met Oliver.

Slipping into bed some time later, she lay back against the
illows, disinclined to pick up her book. Would Oliver ring as
e had done every night for the last week? How did he really
eel about her? She couldn't believe how selfless he was, how

patient, but was that because he really cared or because h
wasn't that affected? He'd certainly felt aroused that evening

Just thinking about touching him, having him touch her, sen
a wave of heat washing through her. She couldn't help bu
wonder what it would be like to go further—what would hav
happened if she hadn't had a second of nervous panic at th
overwhelming but unknown sensations and stopped him. He
body still tingled, her breasts felt sensitive, her blood was stil
zinging through her veins, but she felt a restless tension, a
ache deep inside that needed fulfilment.

She was so lost in reliving all the new experiences that sh
jumped when the phone rang. Smiling, she snuggled down an
reached for the receiver, welcoming the prospect of hearin
Oliver's voice one more time before she slept.

CHAPTER SEVEN

'COME in young man. Let me get a look at you.'

Hiding a smile at the barked command, Oliver walked further into the neat-as-a-pin living room of the bungalow in Gull Close, situated on the other side of the river from Bridge Street. Occupied by Gertrude Stanbury, the former headmistress of the local school, whom everyone had warned him was a tyrant, the home had a small garden beyond the open patio doors and a view of the water. Squatting down to eye level with the rotund figure propped on the sofa by a multitude of pillows, and one each under the knees that were giving her such trouble, he introduced himself.

'Hello, Ms Stanbury, I'm Dr Oliver Fawkner, the new GP.'

'Humph.' One small arthritic hand shook his with a surprisingly strong grip, while sharp grey eyes gave him the once-over. 'You need a haircut. Never would have tolerated that in my school. But you're a handsome devil, I'll say that for you. Are you any good as a doctor?'

The smile he had been trying to hold in escaped. 'Thankfully my other patients seem to think so,' he told her, still holding her hand, taking immediately to the bullish, white-haired lady who was clearly sharp and shrewd and, if the glint in those eyes was anything to go by, had a sense of humour lurking under the surface bluster.

'I suppose you're here to prod and poke me about.'

'And to tell you that we've heard from the hospital. Your operation for the first knee replacement has been brought forward to the third week in September.' Gently, he checked the sixty-seven-year-old over, pleased to find her blood pressure was stable. Aside from the arthritis, which severely reduced her mobility and caused her considerable pain, she appeared to be in good health. 'The consultant will write to you directly but you can always call on us if you need more information or if there is anything else we can do.'

The tyrant-in-disguise patted his hand. 'I'll be glad to get it over and done with.'

'Once you are home again, Lauren Nightingale will be by to help you with some gentle physiotherapy to get you moving and mobile until they can do the second knee,' he explained, sitting back on his heels, taking his time to ensure there was nothing else she needed.

'Talented girl, Lauren,' she muttered with a frown. 'Always good at art. Clumsy as a mule, though, and as stubborn with it. No doubt she'll try and bully me.'

Oliver chuckled. Gertrude Stanbury was priceless! He could just imagine her as the formidable headmistress ruling her school with an iron hand and caring heart. 'Lauren's very good at her job. She'll take care of you. Now, is there anything else I can do for you today? How's the pain?'

'Bloody awful. How do you think?' the woman riposted, but her eyes gleamed and he could tell she was enjoying having someone to spar with.

'I'll take a look at the medications you're on and see if there's anything else that will make you more comfortable until the operation.' Taking both her hands in his, he turned them over and carefully inspected them. 'Any more deterioration with your hands or wrists?'

She looked down, hiding her eyes, but he'd seen the flash of worry in them. 'I get by.'

'We want you to do better than that. I'll investigate some alternative ideas to help you keep active and reduce the pain,' he promised, jotting himself a note on her file. He'd mention it to Lauren, too.

'Would you mind bringing me a fresh jug of chilled water?'

The question was polite but the command was clear nevertheless. 'No problem.' Smiling, Oliver rose to his feet and took the empty jug from the table nearby.

'My daily will have left another one ready in the fridge. Bring yourself a glass. I want to talk to you.'

Checking his watch, Oliver headed to the kitchen. He had one more house call to make before returning to the surgery for his afternoon list and a mountain of paperwork, and while lingering with Ms Stanbury would mean he'd miss lunch, he didn't mind. Having discovered from Lauren that the girls were planning a night out to see some film or other, he'd persuaded Chloe to go and enjoy herself. He'd miss her like crazy, but it was important that she keep up with her own circle of friends.

After last night, when he'd nearly lost the last remnants of his composure, it might be a good idea to cool things for an evening to give him a chance to shore up his ragged self-control before faced with the temptation of Chloe in the flesh again. At least he could look forward to talking with her on the phone at bedtime. Tomorrow, Friday, he was planning a beach picnic after work and the weekly midwifery meeting. If sea conditions permitted, he could do some surfing while Chloe relaxed, then they could eat and talk before he walked her home.

As for the weekend—well, he hoped to spend as much of that with her as possible. Whatever few lingering doubts remained about what he was getting into so soon after his return to Cornwall, he had come too far with Chloe to back off now. Aside from the ever-present physical desire, he genuinely liked her. She made him happy. The more he knew her, the more he agreed with her friends that Chloe was special. When he was with her he felt contented, whole, alive and charged with a buzz of excitement he had never known with anyone else. And he wanted to help her overcome her past.

He took the full jug from the fridge, refilled the empty one and set it in the coolest part to chill before returning to the living room.

'Anything else I can get for you while I'm here, Ms Stanbury?' he asked, handing the woman a glass of fresh, cold water.

'Call me Gertie. And do sit down, young man.'

Oliver grinned. 'Thanks. What did you want to talk to me about?'

'Word has it you're seeing our Chloe.' Shrewd grey eyes assessed him. 'I hope you're not going to break her heart.'

'So do I, Gertie.' Given how deeply he was becoming involved and how little he knew of Chloe's own feelings, he hoped *she* wasn't going to break *his* heart either. Pushing the niggling concern aside, he met Gertie's gaze. 'I shall do everything I can to never hurt Chloe in any way at all.'

The elderly woman gave a satisfied nod. 'I can see you mean it. Good. What that girl needs is someone to cherish her.'

'Do you know Chloe from school?' he asked, unable to resist some gentle prying.

'Yes, indeed. She was a first-class student.' A reminiscent look crossed her face. 'I was so glad to discover how well she had done for herself. When she ran away…'

The words trailed off, but Oliver's gut tightened, his attention sharpening. 'Chloe ran away?'

Gertie paused for a moment, sipping her drink, and Oliver

remained silent, tense and unsettled as he waited, impatient to hear what the woman had to say.

'I don't think anyone knows the extent of what went on in that house.' A shiver ran through her and Oliver felt chilled as the implications of her words sank in. 'I so feared for that poor child. And for her mother. Chloe's father was an evil man.'

'Why did no one do anything?' It was a struggle to keep hold of his temper and disgust at the thought of Chloe and her mother being left at the hands of such a bully.

'There was never any evidence. Chloe's mother denied everything, refused to leave him…Chloe herself would never talk. Too scared to, I suppose, poor mite. Everyone was frightened of him. You hardly ever saw Chloe or her mother outside the house. Thank goodness she was allowed to attend school.' Gertrude shook her head sadly. 'I tried to take an interest in Chloe. As I said, she was an avid learner but she had such a reserve about her and she didn't mix well with people. She ran away when she was sixteen, after her exams. I never knew what happened to her, never expected to see her again, but she must have kept in touch with her mother somehow—I guess through Lauren.'

Sitting forward, Oliver rested his forearms on his knees. 'When did she come back to Penhally?'

'After her father died, four years ago, Chloe returned to care for her mother. She worked locally as a midwife, then joined the surgery when Dr Tremayne and his then partner, Dr Avanti, opened the practice here,' Gertie continued, setting her glass aside, grimacing as she shifted her arthritic body into a more comfortable position. 'When her mother died eighteen months ago, Chloe sold the old house and bought the cottage in Fisherman's Row. I don't know how many people had any inkling back then what went on behind closed doors, or what that girl's life was like. It was well hidden. But I saw enough every day at school to be concerned. My biggest regret is that, although I tried, I couldn't make a difference. Now…well, I am just so proud of Chloe for making a success of herself. She deserves to be happy.'

Oliver felt sick to his stomach. He wanted to tear Chloe's father apart piece by piece—would have done had the man still been alive. Yet even from the grave her father cast a shadow over Chloe's life, one Oliver desperately wanted to lift. He needed Chloe to trust him enough to tell him about her childhood herself. Only then could he really reach her, really begin to help her put the past behind her.

Meeting Gertie's gaze, seeing the understanding in her eyes, he nodded. 'If it's in my power, Gertie, I shall do all I can to make sure Chloe's future is a happy one.'

'A quick word with everyone if I may,' Nick announced standing in the staffroom doorway at the end of a busy Friday

Oliver had left the surgery some while ago to answer an emergency call from the lifeguards to attend an injured tourist on the beach, so Chloe sat next to Lauren. She'd been looking forward to heading home as soon as the midwifery meeting was over, but had been delayed with Rachel Kenner. The girl had needed reassurance and Chloe was trying to see her as often as necessary to give support and advice. Her father was busy with arrangements for the annual remembrance service in August, when the town gathered by the lighthouse in memory of the victims of the storm that had claimed so many lives, Nick's father and brother and Kate's husband James among them.

Chloe was meant to be joining Oliver on the beach for a picnic supper. Given that she had been out with Lauren and Vicky yesterday evening, and today had been so hectic, she had hardly drawn breath, much less spoken with Oliver, she was more than eager to see him. Their phone conversation last night had been brief. She had been late home and sleepy, while he had sounded distracted.

'As you know,' Nick said, his words diverting her from her thoughts, 'I went to France with the twinning committee last weekend. It was a successful visit and things are moving on apace. It should be an excellent venture for Penhally, especially for tourism and business connections. For our part, Dr Gabriel Devereux will be joining us in the practice for a year, and although he won't be able to begin work until autumn, he is coming over shortly for a couple of days to look around. I hope everyone will make him welcome.'

There was some general muttering, but it was one of the practice nurses, Gemma Johnson, who spoke up. 'Have you met him? Does he speak English?'

'His English is perfect—he did some of his training in London—and from all I've heard, he's a highly respected doctor,' Nick confirmed.

His gaze swept the room. Chloe noted how he looked longest at Kate, a frown creasing his brow, the shadows in his eyes suggesting he was still having problems coming to terms with the enormity of the news about her son Jeremiah. *His* son, as it turned out. Chloe wished for a happy ending for them all.

'Dr Devereux will stay with me on this visit, but I've agreed to help him find somewhere suitable to rent. I know Oliver has been comfortable in the flat in Bridge Street, but that was for the short term,' Nick continued, and the reality that Oliver's stay in Penhally might be over all too soon sent a shock wave of alarm and disappointment through Chloe's body. 'If anyone has any ideas, I'd welcome them.'

Lost in thought, Chloe was only half listening as Lauren spoke up. 'What about the Manor House?'

'Isn't that already occupied?' Nick queried.

'Only until the end of August,' Lauren confirmed. 'But the Bartons are going to be away in South Africa for another two years at least. I've heard nothing about new tenants—and given that I live in the Gatehouse Cottage at the end of the drive and have the spare keys, the solicitor always keeps me informed and asks me to check on things. The house is comfortable, furnished, not too grand, and conveniently situated. I'm sure the Bartons would welcome renting it to someone on a year-long let. Especially someone recommended by and attached to the surgery. They are more interested in the quality of the tenant and keeping the house occupied and in good order than in asking for some ridiculously high rent.'

Nick offered a rare smile. 'Thank you, Lauren, that sounds excellent. Could you let me have the contact details for the solicitor? If it can be arranged, and if the house is available, perhaps Dr Devereux can have a look while he is here to see if it will suit his needs.'

'Yes, of course.' Frowning, Lauren reached for her bag and fumbled through it to find her address book. 'I have it here…somewhere.'

'Thank you, everyone,' Nick said. 'Have a good weekend.'

People rose and began filing out, talking among themselves, but Chloe waited for Lauren as they had planned to walk back to town together. Lauren was going to meet Vicky, while Chloe wanted a quick shower and to change her clothes before heading to the surfing beach to find Oliver…and the picnic he had promised her. She was so hungry.

When Lauren was finished and had handed over the details Nick wanted, Chloe turned to leave, noticing Kate ahead of her. She was about to say goodnight when Nick spoke again.

'I appreciate this, Lauren.' His took the piece of paper, then his voice firmed. 'Kate, could you wait a moment? I'd like to have a word.'

Chloe saw the shimmer of wariness in her friend's eyes. 'Yes, of course.'

Hesitating as Lauren went on ahead, Chloe searched Kate's

gaze, feeling anxious about leaving the older woman. But Kate smiled and nodded imperceptibly, and she had no option but to say goodnight and follow Lauren downstairs. Even so, her worry for Kate remained.

Kate tried to appear unconcerned as she was left alone with Nick. True, since she had confronted him at home he had been civil to her at work, but the tension remained between them. Their old friendship was in tatters. She tried so hard to understand him; despite all the upset, blame and guilt over Annabel's death, Kate was sure that Nick had still not properly grieved for his wife. On top of which he had found out about Jem in the worst of ways. She wished that had never happened but it was too late to turn back the clock. And however unrequited her love, however hopeless the situation seemed, she could not regret having Jem in her life.

Meeting Nick's watchful gaze, she struggled for composure. 'You wished to talk to me,' she prompted, managing to keep her voice level.

'Yes. Sit, please.' She did as she had been bidden, while Nick closed the door and then sat opposite her, looking uncomfortable. Legs braced, he rested his elbows on his knees, his hands clenched together. 'I know it's rich of me to ask, given the recent difficulties between us, but you have been—and still are—invaluable to the practice.'

'Thank you.'

The praise surprised her. Nick was not often one for compliments or showing his feelings. That he had said anything, especially in the current circumstances, created a warm glow inside her.

'I know your role here has changed since you ceased being practice manager and returned to midwifery, but I would be grateful if you would be among the few to come for lunch to meet Dr Devereux, to welcome him and help familiarise him with the practice and Penhally Bay.'

Kate swallowed her disappointment. She should have known Nick would only want to talk with her about work. 'I see. Who else will be there?'

'I was thinking of asking Dragan and Melinda. As incomers themselves, and originally from continental Europe, I thought they might have useful insights for Gabriel.'

'That's a good idea,' she acknowledged, realising how hard Nick was trying, that this was important to him—and maybe important to them in the longer term.

'Lucy and Ben will be coming, too, and bringing baby Annabel. I want to keep it informal. A barbecue, I thought. I…' The hesitation lengthened, then he raised his head, the expression in his eyes cautious. 'I have no objection if you wish to bring Jeremiah.'

Kate sat back, considering his words. Jem would attend as *her* son—she read that much between the lines. Part of her was downhearted, and yet she recognised the gesture for what it was…an olive branch of sorts. She couldn't expect too much too soon. Maybe if Nick saw Jem again in a social setting he would feel some draw, even if he was far from ready to acknowledge him as his son. It was less than she had dreamed of, but more than she had hoped for in recent weeks, so she accepted the hesitant step forward.

'All right, Nick,' she agreed, calling herself all kinds of a fool for allowing his answering smile to affect her so. 'We'll be happy to come and meet Gabriel.'

'Thank you, Kate, I appreciate it. I'll let you know when I have confirmation for the date of his visit.'

The edge of relief in his tone and the slight relaxing of his tension gave her a measure of hope that the future might not be as bleak as she had feared.

* * *

Chloe sat on the sand, her arms around her drawn-up knees, enjoying the early evening sunshine and the sight of Oliver surfing. Even though the beach was still busy and many people were in the water, she had picked him out straight away, instinctively drawn to him, admiring even from this distance the impressive athleticism of his six-foot-three inch frame, his supple movements, as if he were at one with the waves. The swell wasn't huge, but he caught the next crest, twisting, turning, weaving, as he rode the board back towards the shore. Moments later, he was wading through the shallows, his board tucked under his arm, his free hand pushing wet strands of hair back from his face.

Oh, my! Chloe thought she might self-destruct at the sight of him. All that bare, olive-toned skin over lean muscle dotted with water droplets. Strong shoulders, broad chest with a light dusting of dark hair arrowing down in a narrow line over an impressive abdomen, tight belly and disappearing under the low-slung, body-moulding, wetsuit shorts he wore. And she could glimpse part of the second tattoo he had mentioned. Sited off-centre, below his navel and over his right hipbone, the top of it peeped out from the waistband of his shorts. She couldn't distinguish what it was but, remembering how wonderful it had been to touch him two nights ago, she was filled with an eagerness to explore that body further.

Finding it hard to draw breath, Chloe struggled to swallow the lump lodged in her throat when her gaze clashed with his. His lips parted, his eyes darkened, and then he smiled. That slow, sexy, dimpled smile that melted her insides and made her forget her own name. He dropped to his knees beside her and leaned in to give her a lingering kiss.

'Hi, babe.'

'Hi.' He smelt of sea, sun and man. 'Sorry I'm late. Nick held us all back to talk about the twinning thing. Some French

doctor is coming over in a few months to work in the practice
for a year.'

'Yeah?'

Oliver seemed interested but not concerned, and her fertile
imagination conjured up reasons why the arrival of an extra
doctor didn't bother him. Was there room at the surgery for
both Oliver and Gabriel? Was Oliver planning to extend his
current contract? She had taken Kate's advice and had asked
Oliver about his return to Cornwall. He'd been open about his
desire for a different kind of life, his need to settle, and she had
hoped that had meant he would stay in Penhally itself.

She had also been surprised and moved that someone as
self-assured and confident as Oliver had insecurities about
himself. He'd explained how he had never been able to shake
off the playboy reputation or the family name, that people
judged him on those rather than the person he was. She had
felt guilty because that was exactly how she *had* first seen him.
Now, though, she thought of him very differently. And she
didn't want him to leave. As she was struggling with her
confused emotions, her stomach gave an audible rumble and
Oliver laughed, rising to his feet again.

'Sounds like I need to feed you,' he teased, picking up his
surfboard. 'The car is nearby so I'll head back to fetch the
cooler. I won't be long.'

'OK.'

Chloe watched him go, admiring his rear view. Sighing, she
dropped her head on her knees, thinking about comments made
by Vicky last night when they had been out at the cinema.
Comments she had tried to banish from her mind.

'I sometimes wonder if there's any oestrogen in your body,'
Vicky had complained.

Taken aback, Chloe had frowned. 'What do you mean?'

'Well, you have the scrumptious Oliver Fawkner panting
after you and you don't seem to be doing anything about it.'

Warming to her theme—subtle and tactful not being in her vo-cabulary—Vicky had continued. 'A holiday fling is what you need. No commitment, just some fun with a guy who knows how to please a woman. I'll have him if you don't want him!'

Vicky's words upset her now as they had last night. Lauren had intervened, and had later taken her aside and told her to take no notice. 'You know what Vicky is like. She doesn't mean any harm. And she doesn't know about your past.'

Which was true, Chloe acknowledged now. But she didn't want to think of her relationship with Oliver as some mean-ingless fling, and she was worried because she had no idea how *he* viewed their time together. She had no experience of this kind of thing, her feelings were so new and beyond her under-standing. After Vicky's comments, and now with the news that Gabriel Devereux would be coming from France, she couldn't shake off the nagging fear that Oliver might not be serious about her, that he might move on. From her if not from Penhally itself.

'What's wrong?'

She glanced up, so lost in thought she had been unaware of Oliver's return. 'Nothing,' she answered, managing a smile, her gaze travelling over him.

He had changed out of his wetsuit into ordinary cut-off denims, topped with a short-sleeved shirt he had left unbut-toned, allowing her a glimpse of his delectable torso. Her hands itched to explore him again. Her own body yearned to feel his touch. Setting the cooler down, he sat beside her and began taking out an impressive array of food. The sight of the treats in store, including some of the Trevellyans' blue cheese she loved so much, had her stomach rumbling again.

She felt a new edginess, a tension, as if they had reached a turning point. But maybe that was inside herself. She had deci-sions to make, and she knew if she wanted to take things further with Oliver she needed to face up to the demons that held her back. For now, though, she would enjoy his company and their picnic…time enough later to gather the courage to confront her memories of her father and confide in Oliver about her past.

The picnic had been a success and, as always, he adored being with Chloe. But Oliver sensed something had been different this evening. At times she had seemed distracted, focused inward, and a flicker of unease gripped him as he followed her inside her cottage. For a moment she stood with her back to him, looking out of the window, and he couldn't wait any longer to hold her. Closing the distance between them, admiring her curves in her sleeveless, knee-length dress, he slid his arms around her waist, nuzzling her neck as he drew her back against him.

'You're very quiet tonight, babe.'

'Just a bit tired,' she murmured. 'It's been a hectic week.'

He frowned, not entirely convinced by her explanation. 'Do you want me to go home and let you get an early night?' He'd be disappointed to cut short his time with her but he didn't want her fatigued.

'No.' She wriggled in his hold, turning to face him, taking him by surprise when she wrapped her arms around his waist and buried her face against him, her words muffled. 'No, don't go.'

Something wasn't right. He tightened his hold, raising a hand to stroke her hair. 'I missed this last night.'

'Me, too.'

'But you had a good time?' he asked, hearing an edge in her voice.

She burrowed closer against him. 'It was fine.'

'Did someone upset you?'

'No.' He didn't believe her but she changed the subject before he could question her further. 'What have you been up to the last couple of days?'

'Actually, I met an old friend of yours,' he told her, deciding to take a chance and offer her an opening to confide in him.

She pulled back to look up at him. 'You did? Who?'

'Gertie.'

'Gertie?' He smiled because her puzzled frown looked so cute. 'I don't know a Gertie.'

'Gertrude Stanbury. Your old headmistress.'

This time he laughed aloud at the expression on Chloe's face, her eyes widening, her mouth dropping open in shock. 'You called Ms Stanbury *Gertie*?'

'She asked me to. She likes me.'

'Obviously.' Chloe shook her head, a genuine smile curving her mouth. 'You're such a charmer!'

He manufactured a hurt look. 'What did I do?'

'We were so in awe of her at school,' she reflected with a reminiscent frown. 'Her rule was law. Nothing got by her.'

'She did say I should have a haircut.'

'I bet!'

Oliver regarded her for a moment. 'You think I should cut my hair?'

'No!' She sounded horrified at the prospect, but his smile faded as her fingers sank into the thick strands at his nape, tightening his gut and increasing his arousal. 'I like it. I just meant Ms Stanbury would have commented on it.'

'Yeah, she had quite a bit to say for herself. She's very fond of you,' he added, watching her carefully, controlling his own emotions as he recalled the tale the older lady had related.

'Really?'

'Mmm.' He slipped his hand under the fall of her hair and trailed his fingers over her silken skin. 'She said she used to worry about you, and she's very proud of your success.'

A welter of emotions chased across Chloe's green eyes, ranging from alarm to surprise. 'Oh. What else did she say?'

she queried, a new wariness in her voice, her body tensing in his hold, her arms loosening from around him.

'She told me how much she regretted being unable to help you, to make a difference. She said you ran away.'

'Yes.' He could feel her trembling before she moved away from him, wrapping her arms around herself. 'No one could have helped.'

Oliver was disappointed by her withdrawal, even though he had expected it. He felt nervous himself, concerned he was pushing too fast, unsure how best to reach Chloe, to encourage her to open up to him, to convince her it was safe to do so. Taking her hand, he led her to the sofa and sat down. Expecting her to keep her distance, he was relieved and delighted when she cuddled up against him.

'My father was a controlling, vindictive man.' Oliver held his breath as Chloe began speaking, wanting to protect her, hoping he was strong enough to help her through what was to come. Cradling her head on his shoulder, he kissed the top of her head. 'I don't know what had turned him that way but he was paranoid about things and he had very set rules and ideas. Nothing was ever good enough for him. The slightest thing would send him into a rage.'

'Was he an alcoholic?'

Chloe shook her head, turning more fully into him, her hand resting on his chest. 'No. He didn't need a drink to lose his head, to be violent. He did have a drink, on occasion, but not often. He had cut my mother off from her family and friends before I was even born. I don't know if I have grandparents, cousins or anything.'

'Why did he do that?' he asked when she paused, his fingers tracing soothing circles on the back of her neck.

'Like I said, it was all about control. He brought her here when they married. She knew no one, wasn't allowed to work, to go out without him, to have friends. He had to be in charge of her whole life. And mine when I came along,' she added, a quiver in her voice, and Oliver closed his eyes. 'He was physically, emotionally and verbally abusive to us both…sexually abusive to my mother.'

'But not to you?' He didn't know how to get the words past the painful lump in his throat.

'Not to me. Not that,' she confirmed softly.

A sigh of relief escaped him. Not that the rest she had suffered hadn't been bad enough. He couldn't bear to think of Chloe left vulnerable at the hands of such a man—her own father who was meant to protect and nurture her.

'What happened, Chloe?'

'Sometimes, when I was very young, if he decided I'd been bad, he'd lock me in a cupboard, often for hours. Later he'd use his fists,' she admitted, and he could hear the remembered fear and pain behind her words.

'Didn't your mother do anything to protect you?' Despite seeing cases during his medical career, knowing of people who stayed with their abusers for various reasons, he didn't have his rational doctor head on now because this was Chloe and personal, and he felt angry, aching for her. 'Why didn't she leave him?'

Chloe drew in a ragged breath and he shifted them so they were lying on the sofa and he could hold her more securely, keeping her close and safe. 'I feel bad, guilty, because I often hated her, blamed her for staying,' she whispered, and he felt the wetness of her tears seep through his shirt.

'No, babe,' he protested, desperate to get through to her, to not have her carry this burden. 'They were the adults. Their responsibility, their duty, was to care for you. You have nothing to feel guilty about.'

For a few moments a tense silence stretched, and he wondered if she would continue, if he could bear it if she did. They had not turned the light on and, as dusk fell, the darkening room gave a privacy that appeared to encourage the sharing of secrets.

'I think my mother was so brainwashed, her self-esteem so shattered, that she couldn't think for herself,' Chloe explained, a deep sigh torn from her. 'She said she loved him once, that it was her duty as his wife, that you made allowances, even that he didn't mean it. But he *did* mean it.' Anger and disgust rang in her voice. 'He enjoyed the control, the domination. His rules were strict and often contradictory. He demanded that my mother remain feminine and attractive for him, yet he criticised her for her appearance and accused her of trying to attract other men.' Almost by instinct, she pressed closer, as if seeking the comfort he was so desperate to give her. 'Once I became a teenager, his anger focused more on me, on putting me down, challenging me, finding fault. Apart from school, I wasn't allowed out. I couldn't have friends, wear nice clothes, make-up, jewellery, perfume. Then he started accusing me of flaunting myself for men, of being just like my mother.'

'Chloe…' Her name escaped as a groan. He felt helpless, unable to imagine the horror her life had been, furious that no one had helped her. And he could see how the groundwork had been laid to make Chloe subconsciously deny her sexuality and attractiveness—and mistrust men. 'Was there no one you could talk to?'

She shook her head. 'He had us so well isolated. And he made it clear what he would do if we ever told anyone. I hated him, Oliver, and while I felt sorry for my mother, wanted to stop her pain, I began to hate her, too, to disrespect her for not doing anything. And yet I did nothing myself, was just as cowardly and afraid of him.'

'What could you have done on your own? As a child, with no adults stepping in to care for you?' he interjected. 'Don't blame yourself, babe, please. It is not your fault. And you most definitely were not, and are not, a coward.'

He understood now why Chloe's past experiences made her wary and cynical about relationships, love, marriage, men. Frightened, she had protected herself by shutting down the part of her that would allow desire, believing it led to hurt and abuse and the surrendering of control, of her very self. He was angry and distressed at all she had endured, but so proud of her for all she had achieved despite it, for having the courage to face it, to share it with him, to let him close to her. It was a special gift, one he hoped he deserved. To know he was the first man she had ever trusted, had ever allowed to kiss her, hold her, touch her… It was humbling, overwhelming.

'What happened to make you run away?' he asked, his voice rough with emotion.

He felt her shaking and hated himself for causing her any further upset. 'It was after my exams, when I was sixteen. I came home from school to find my father waiting for me. He started accusing me, saying he had seen me flirting with a man outside school. It was crazy. I'd spoken to a boy, a classmate, about an exam for less than a minute, but nothing I said made a difference. You didn't answer back, didn't challenge his perception of things. He…' She halted, her voice breaking.

'It's OK,' he whispered, his chest tight, stroking a hand up and down her back. 'You don't have to tell me.'

'I do. I need to.' Oliver's own shuddering breath mirrored hers. 'He said I had to be taught a lesson.' Again she paused and he heard the determination in her voice. Turning more onto his back he drew her on top of him and she pressed her face into his neck. 'It was Lauren who found me hiding after I had escaped his attack. She and Vicky were three years ahead of me at school, so not really friends with me then. Lauren had left home after A levels, moving away to do her physiotherapy training, but she was back for a week's break. I was a mess. Bleeding and bruised. He'd hacked all my hair off with scissors. I was so scared, so angry. I felt guilty leaving my mother, but I knew I could never go back there. I believed he'd kill me one day.'

'God, Chloe.' Shocked, his hold tightened and he wished he had been around to protect her, get her away.

'Lauren took me to her home. Thankfully her parents were out. Did you know she was adopted?' she asked, confusing him for a moment with the change of tack.

'No,' he admitted, getting his head together. 'I didn't know that.'

'Anyway, Lauren cleaned my cuts, found me clothes, fed me, got part of the story out of me. Then she gave me money, made some phone calls to a women's group she knew through college, and found me a safe place to stay away from Penhally. No one else knew where I had gone, at least to begin with, but I kept in touch with Lauren and she passed on news about my mother. The shelter helped me get on my feet and find a way to pursue my goal to be a midwife. When I was twenty-three, I heard my father had died and that my mother needed someone. I came back and felt strangely detached. I couldn't grieve for him, and I had confused, ambivalent feelings for her, but I needed to do it, needed the closure. She was a broken woman, her mind was scattered, hardly in touch with reality. We never talked about what happened. As for Lauren, I returned the money eventually, but I can never repay her for all the rest.'

'You are amazing, babe. Strong and brave.'

'No, it was just self-preservation,' she refuted, sounding sad. 'Years ago my mother told me I'd understand one day. But I'm never going to be like her, never going to endure what she did for love.'

Her words troubled him and showed him the journey was not yet over. Cupping her face with his hands, he tried to see her in the darkness, to give her his strength, assure her he was sincere, prove to her she could trust him.

'That wasn't love, Chloe. Not at all. You're not your mother…and I'm not your father.'

She didn't answer, but neither did she pull away. Instead, she rested her head on his chest and slipped her arms around him. He held her long into the night, seeking guidance for the best way to help her, stunned, overcome, even more in awe and in love with her than he had been before she had trusted him with the horrors of her childhood.

For a moment he froze, realising what he had just admitted to himself. He hadn't planned it, hadn't expected it to happen so soon, but this whole gamut of feelings and emotions had grown and deepened over the weeks and he was in love with Chloe MacKinnon. In some ways he was stepping into the unknown as much as she was, experiencing all this for the first time. Chloe deserved the best—he prayed that could be him.

He felt the full weight of responsibility for what he was taking on, for what this meant for Chloe's sake. But he knew with an utter certainty and finality that he didn't just want to be the first man Chloe let into her life, he wanted to be the *only* man. The man to claim her heart, the man to cherish her and love her and care for her…for ever.

If only she would let him.

CHAPTER EIGHT

HER Saturday lunch-time parents' class over, Chloe headed out to Lauren's cottage and wandered around her studio, admiring the selection of paintings her friend had available for sale. When she decided which one she wanted, there would be the usual good-natured debate about the cost, an argument Chloe was always determined to win, convinced that Lauren should not make over-generous allowances for her friends. In truth, she loved all Lauren's work, but this painting had to be extra-special because it was for Oliver.

Just thinking about him made her warm and tingly, although thoughts of last night, of facing up to the past and revealing the full extent of her father's cruelty, had a chilling effect. Confiding in Oliver had been one of the most difficult things she had ever done. Not because of the way Oliver had reacted. Far from it. He had been wonderful…tender, considerate, protective and supportive. She had felt his anger, but it had been *for* her, and she had never felt anything but safe with him.

For the second time she had fallen asleep in his arms, only to wake up that morning to find herself alone on the sofa, a light throw tucked around her, a pillow under her head, and his note propped on the coffee-table, waiting for her. She'd had appointments and her lunchtime class, while Oliver had had morning surgery, so she had not seen him yet today, but she had done a lot of thinking.

That he believed in her made her feel good, and thinking of his words, his reasoning, had helped ease her long-buried guilt. Oliver was right. None of it had been her fault. Her parents had failed in their responsibilities to protect her. She had not been to blame for her father's anger, or for her mother's choices. Sharing the burden with Oliver, telling him things she had never told anyone else, not even Lauren, had brought unexpected but welcome inner peace, a letting go. She refused to allow her father any more influence on the rest of her life.

She wanted to do something for Oliver to show her appreciation. Something tangible that, should he decide to leave, would be a reminder of her and his time in Penhally. That he might go was too painful to consider. It would soon be his birthday and, knowing how he admired Lauren's work and loved the local landscape, it had seemed an excellent idea to buy one of her paintings for him.

'Have you found something you like?' Lauren asked with a smile, handing her a glass of chilled fruit juice.

'Thanks.' Chloe took a sip of the drink and turned back to the array of work with a sigh. 'I love them all. That's the trouble.'

Her friend laughed. 'I appreciate the compliment. Perhaps I can help. Where are you going to hang it?'

'Actually, I'm not. It's a present…for Oliver,' she admitted, blushing.

'Really?' Lauren's smile widened. 'That's great. I'm so pleased for you, Chloe.'

'It's his birthday in two weeks' time. I want to thank him— and I want him to have something to remember me by if he leaves Penhally.'

Lauren frowned. 'What makes you think he might leave? He wants to settle down, doesn't he?'

'He's said nothing about staying or extending his contract at the surgery.' Sitting down, she confided her fears to her friend. 'I told him about Gabriel Devereux arriving from France in the autumn, and Oliver wasn't the least bothered.'

'The surgery is getting busier all the time, especially with the ongoing expansion, and could easily carry another GP or two. Lucy is still on maternity leave and Dragan will be cutting back when Melinda has the baby. And with Ed and Maddy having recently chosen hospital work in St Piran over staying at the practice, there is space for Oliver and, later, the French doctor for his year's placement. Probably another nurse, too. You're really smitten with Oliver, aren't you?' Lauren added after a pause, sitting beside her.

'Yes.' Chloe met her friend's gaze. 'But I don't know how he feels. And I have no experience of this sort of thing. What if Vicky's right and this is just a fling?'

Lauren waved her comment aside. 'Vicky was talking nonsense, and you know it. Oliver cares about you, Chloe. We can all see it. And we can all see the difference in you, too. You're blossoming. It's fantastic. You've come such a long way in the last days and weeks. Don't get cold feet and turn back now. Oliver is good for you—and believe me, you're good for him. See where it takes you, go for what you want.'

'I don't know.'

'Hasn't he shown you how different he is? Has he ever pressured you, scared you, tried to change or control you? Has he ever said he's leaving?'

Confused, Chloe shook her head. It was true that Oliver made her feel things she had never felt before. Things that were so unfamiliar but which made her heart beat with excitement and brought incredible sensations to her body. But he had always left the choice to her, had respected her, never pressured her.

'What I feel is scary…but exciting,' she admitted.

'You are learning what it is to be a woman, desired by a sexy man. Go with it. You won't be sorry,' Lauren reassured. 'Now, about this picture.'

Dragging her thoughts back to the matter at hand, Chloe stood up again and returned her attention to the canvases. 'Are you trying some new techniques?' she asked, noting subtle differences in Lauren's new work compared with older pictures.

'No, why?'

Surprised at the edge in her friend's voice, Chloe glanced round and saw Lauren frowning in puzzlement, almost squinting as she looked at her own work. A flicker of unease curled inside her as she remembered Oliver's questions about Lauren's clumsiness. Could there really be something wrong? Unwilling to consider it, sure her friend would say something if there was a problem, Chloe tried to set her disquiet aside. Perhaps she was seeing changes in the paintings that weren't there.

'All the pictures are amazing, Lauren. But with Oliver's love of the sea, I'll settle on this magnificent coastal landscape,' she decided, preparing herself for the battle ahead to ensure Lauren took enough money for her work.

Oliver glanced at his watch and wondered when Chloe would be home. He hadn't seen her since last night, when leaving her had been almost impossible. After a busy morning at the surgery, when his clinic had overrun he had sent her a text and discovered she was with Lauren for the afternoon and having a meal with her friend. Having told her he was home if she wanted to meet up, all he could do was wait. And worry. He understood if she was feeling awkward after last night's talk about her past and knew she might need some space. But he wanted to be with her. He still felt shaky, sick about all she had suffered, angry that no one had helped her. Until Lauren. Thank goodness she had been there to help Chloe get away to safety.

As for his own feelings for Chloe, well, he loved and wanted her more every day. He had never spent so much time with a woman, being with her, getting to know her, talking, laughing, dating…all without sex getting in the way. He enjoyed it. Because it was Chloe. Not that he didn't want to make love with her. He did. He ached for it, and hoped they'd get there before he expired from unfulfilled desire. In the meantime, everything about her fascinated him, and the slow build-up of the physical side of things was exciting, and heightened the anticipation.

That she had been completely unaware of her own body's needs and desires was amazing, but awakening her to intimacy, sharing the journey with her, was the most incredible experience of his life, an honour and a privilege. He could kiss and touch Chloe for ever. Yearned to do so. It took every atom of self-control he had not to rush things. Tamping down his desire, his urgent need to know her fully, wasn't easy, but he was determined to do this the right way for Chloe. Nothing had ever felt this special. Being with Chloe made his world a better place. He wanted her, needed her. But it was too soon to tell her. He had to be sure of her feelings for him and where she saw this going before he made a public commitment. What scared him was that Chloe might never be ready to consider love, marriage and for ever.

He paced the small rented flat. In a week or so he would have to vacate it, make long-term plans about work and living arrangements. He glanced at his watch again. Was Chloe home yet? Should he ring her? He dragged his fingers through his hair, caught in an agony of indecision yet knowing the next move had to be hers.

Chloe stored Oliver's painting safely in her spare room. The end of July was approaching. She hoped he would stay, but what would happen if he didn't? What if he left and she never experienced being with him in the fullest sense of the word because she had been too cautious, too cowardly to take a chance and go for what she knew deep down inside she wanted?

She couldn't imagine ever feeling like this about anyone else. Couldn't imagine ever allowing any other man into her life the way she had Oliver. Because she trusted him. Trusted him not to be like her father, not to hurt her, control her, abuse her. If she gave herself to him now, he would take a big piece of her heart and soul if he left, and she might never be the same again. But if she didn't… Lauren was right. No one knew what tomorrow would bring. And she would forever regret this missed opportunity if she didn't take it.

Her mind made up, she left her cottage, thankful not to meet anyone as she made her way to Oliver's flat. As she walked, she thought over the last weeks, the way she had grown in confidence thanks to Oliver's patient care. They had progressed from those first awkward kisses, when she hadn't known what to do, to the most amazingly erotic, deep, drugging kisses that knocked her senseless and set every part of her aflame. Then there had been some pretty serious petting. She felt hot and achy just thinking about his touch…and being able to touch him.

Despite rejecting Vicky's ridiculous suggestion that she use Oliver for sexual experimentation, Chloe *was* curious. Not because she wanted to see what sex was like on a general level, and certainly not to use Oliver. She could never do that. This was about Oliver himself, the need she felt for him alone. The thought of stepping into the unknown was scary. But she had reached the point where she was even more scared *not* to explore where this might go. He had awakened a long-dormant part of her. It was him she wanted. Badly.

Shaking with nerves, she hesitated outside Oliver's door, reaching out to ring the door bell before her remaining courage deserted her. It was several moments before she heard the turn of the lock, then the door opened. She had been on the point of walking away, losing her nerve, but she froze, her gaze locked on Oliver, taking in the wonder of the man. She looked slowly up long, tanned, muscled legs to where a pair of skimpy, faded denim shorts hung low on narrow hips, the button unfastened. The tattoo above one hip bone was almost fully visible—vaguely it registered that it depicted a lone wolf. Her gaze followed the narrow line of dark hair from the gaping waistband, up over a taut belly and toned abdomen to the perfectly contoured chest, broad and muscled, olive skin marked by the two orbs of bronze nipples.

Slowly, he raised one arm and braced it on the doorframe above his head, the rippling play of muscles and the tattoo banding his bicep distracting her. She felt hot enough to melt into a puddle at his feet and couldn't drag enough air into her lungs. Biting her lip, she forced her gaze to continue up the strong column of his throat, over a jaw darkened with the shadow of a day's stubble, past sensual lips that held such sexy promise until her gaze clashed with his. Rich brown eyes…sinful, liquid, hot with a sexual need that both excited and frightened her. Part of her wanted to run away. The rest of her couldn't move, wanted to stay, needed to touch him.

'Chloe?'

The smoky voice pushed her over the edge. She pressed a closed fist to her sternum, terrified she was going to hyperventilate or faint or do something equally embarrassing in front of him. A ragged breath shuddered through her.

'Is something wrong, babe?'

She shook her head, unable to speak. Vulnerable, she tried to convey through her eyes why she was here. Her heart rate doubled as awareness stilled him. His own eyes darkened impossibly, his expression growing hotter, even more intense, and his lips parted a fraction as if in silent invitation and anticipation. He said nothing, just lowered his arm and held out his hand to her. Trembling so badly she could barely command her limbs to obey, she took a jerky step forward and placed her hand in his, sealing her fate.

Warm, strong fingers closed over hers and drew her inexorably closer. She stepped over the threshold, deafened by the pulse racing in her ears, drawn by the unquenchable ache deep inside her. The sound of the door closing and the lock turning was loud in the electrically charged silence.

Helpless to halt her own fate, Chloe surrendered herself to Oliver's will.

Oliver couldn't believe that Chloe was there, that she had come to him, but he read the need in her eyes, felt it in the quiver of her body, the frantic race of her pulse. He wanted her as he had wanted no other woman. He ached with it, ached to back her up to the wall and take her, hot, hard and desperately. But he knew he couldn't do that. Not yet. Somehow he had to get a grip on his raging desire before it slipped out of control. This was Chloe's first time, and whatever it cost him to wait and go slowly, so be it. He was going to make this as special and memorable an experience for her as he could. Later there would be time to indulge in more carnal, urgent pursuits and introduce her to exciting new experiences. Later...

Not yet breaking the silence between them, he led her to his bedroom, more than grateful he'd stocked up on some condoms in the last few days in the hope that this precious event might happen. His hand held hers lightly. He wanted her to join him of her own free will, to make the decision herself. As much as he longed to sweep her up in his arms and tumble her to his bed to ravish her, this had to be Chloe's choice. The first time had to be right. Halting beside the bed, he turned to face her, his heart swelling with affection at the look in her eyes...a sliver of fear mixed with determination and longing. He was so damn proud of her.

'Are you sure this is what you want, Chloe?'

'Y-yes. If you do.'

'Hell, yes!' Feeling raw with need, he gave a rough laugh at her doubt. 'You have no idea how badly. But this time is for you, babe. If I do anything you don't like, you tell me. If you want me to stop, you say so. OK?'

She gave a shaky nod. 'OK.'

Holding her gaze, he released her hand and slowly began to undo the buttons down the front of her sleeveless, multi-coloured sundress. 'First we'll get this off you. I can't wait to see you properly. You're so beautiful, Chloe. I want to touch you and taste you all over. You always remind me of food,' he murmured, brushing his lips along her neck.

'Food?'

'Mmm.' He nuzzled against her, his tongue flicking out to sample her skin. 'You smell like green apples, sunshine and fresh air. Your skin is as smooth and pure as cream, you taste as sweet as honey, and your mouth and nipples are as succulent and juicy as strawberries. I want to eat you all up, Chloe. I hunger for you…and it's never going to stop. You are a feast I shall never have my fill of.'

'Oliver…' Her whole body trembled in reaction to his words.

'Let me love you, babe. Let me show you how beautiful you are, how special desire and passion and making love will be between us.'

'Yes.'

She whimpered, swaying as he peeled off the dress and discarded it, revealing her lush curves covered only in lacy green bra and panties. Heat seared through him. His nostrils flared. Sucking in a strangled breath, he fought to keep to the plan, despite how painfully hard and desperate he was for her. To distract himself and boost her confidence, he kept talking to her, praising her. His own hand shook as he reached out and traced the outline of her bra and panties with his fingertips, watching and feeling the reactions of her body to the light touches. A flush of arousal warmed soft, ivory skin, her nipples hardened further, pushing anxiously against their lace covering, and her flesh rippled as she shivered in anticipation.

'You can touch me, too, Chloe. I want you to. I long to feel your hands and mouth on me.'

Guiding her palms to his chest, he left her to explore, loving her curious, enthusiastic touch. He reached round to unfasten her bra, allowing the perfection of her breasts to spill free. Full, firm but soft, they filled his hands and she moaned as he shaped them, his thumbs grazing over the tight, swollen, sensitive peaks. She arched towards him in response, her own fingers tightening on his flesh.

Chloe was so reactive to his touch. He couldn't wait to turn weeks of seductive kisses and lingering foreplay into the real thing, imagining how much pleasure he could bring her. Resisting the temptation to linger on her breasts just yet, he knelt in front of her, sliding his hands down her hips. Leaning in, he nuzzled the rounded swell of her belly, breathing in the scent of her. His heart thudded, his body tightened even further. Slipping his hands round to cup her delicious rear, he held her still for him as he explored her navel with lips, teeth and tongue. She gasped, squirming against him, and he felt her legs giving way. Supporting her, he eased down her panties, his gaze drawn to ivory thighs and the apex of them where a triangle of soft dark curls arrowed down to the core of her femininity. He laid her gently on the bed, moving to straddle her, his knees on either side of hers, keeping his shorts on to maintain some much-needed distance so he remembered this was for Chloe and didn't end things in an instant.

Running his hands up her body, he leaned in to kiss her, giving her more of his weight, rubbing his chest across her breasts as she wrapped her arms around him and opened her mouth for his tongue. She tasted amazing. His own body shook as her hands tentatively explored, her nails grazing down his spine, threatening to tip him over the edge. He drew back, concentrating on her needs.

His fingers stroked the baby-soft skin of her thighs, sliding higher as they parted for him, dipping between, feeling her heat and growing excitement. Her hold on him tightened and he drew his head back to watch her, seeing the flush of arousal colour her face, her eyes turning darker and unfocused. Her breaths were rapid and ragged as he brushed his fingers over her, getting her used to the sensations before touching her more intimately. She felt incredible. He sucked in his own shuddering breath, sure he was going up in flames at any moment.

'Oliver?'

She sounded uncertain at what she was feeling. 'Easy, babe,' he soothed, taking his time as he stroked her, slowly parting her and exploring deeper.

Unbelievable. She was perfect. So hot and wet. And tight, he discovered as he carefully pressed one finger inside her. He used the pad of his thumb to circle and brush across her sensitive clitoris, and she gasped, squirming on the bed, clutching at him.

'What…? What's happening?' she cried on a half-sob.

'Trust me. Just let go.' She was so close. He could feel it in her, the building tension. Carefully he added a second finger, rhythmically stroking inside her. 'Go with it, Chloe. Let it happen. It feels good, doesn't it?'

'Yes! Please…Oliver!'

She tightened round his fingers and he took her through the release that gripped her, holding her close, revelling in the cries pulled from her as she clung to him, surrendering to what he knew was the first climax she had ever experienced. He made sure to extend and prolong the sensations for her,

Watching her pleasure was incredible. It overwhelmed him to share this with her, to know he was the one to make her feel good, to make her come apart. And this was just the beginning.

Easing his fingers from her, he softly stroked her trembling thighs and belly, brushing kisses across her flushed face. 'You were amazing, babe. Did you like it?'

Nodding she turned her face into his neck, hiding, her arms wrapping around him.

'Don't be shy with me.' Her flesh quivered as his fingers resumed their light stroking along her inner thighs. 'What you felt that time will only get better, Chloe. When I use my mouth on you. When I'm inside you and we come together.'

He gave her a few moments to adjust, then he began kissing her again, building up her arousal a step at a time as he slowly inched his hands and his mouth down her body, worshipping every part of her, lingering at her breasts before continuing his journey to her navel, then lower. She froze in shock the first time he touched his mouth to her most intimate flesh but he gentled her through, encouraged by the responses of her body, her sighs and moans, the way she writhed beneath him.

'You can't,' she gasped in shocked delight.

Oliver chuckled. 'Sure I can.' And he proceeded to show her how.

'Oh, my! Oliver!'

'Come for me, babe.'

He kept her on the brink for as long as his patience could bear it, then led her over the edge to her second orgasm, this one even stronger and more intense than the first. He kept his tongue and fingers moving, intensifying her pleasure, loving her cries, her uninhibited responses. As after-shocks rippled through her, he released her long enough to shrug out of his shorts and reach for a condom, cursing his shaking fingers as he wrestled to extract it and roll it on. Soon it would be time.

He'd needed Chloe to climax a couple of times, wanted her

so hot and wet and needy that she would be relaxed and boneless enough that she wouldn't have the time to worry or the strength to tense herself when he took her virginity. He was scared. He'd never been anyone's first man before. He didn't want to hurt her, ever, and he'd tried everything he could think of to make it as easy and good for her as possible. She had been so tight to his fingers and he shook with wanting, imagining how it would feel to be inside her. Chloe was so special. Looking down at her, limp and replete, a small smile curving her mouth, he knew it was now or never.

Chloe struggled to open her eyes as she felt Oliver's hands lift her sated body and slide a pillow under her hips before gently setting her down again. Why was he doing that? His fingers stroked her thighs, parting them before he eased between them. She felt languid, every part of her quivering with sensation after the indescribable pleasure of two amazing orgasms, and it took an effort to raise her hand and run her fingers up his chest and throat to cup his jaw. The faint rasp of stubble was an exciting caress against her skin. His earthy male scent teased her, aroused her. Heat shimmered off him and she met his gaze, saw the intent in his eyes, the flare of colour across his cheek-bones.

Oh, help. It was going to happen.

She wanted it, but she was scared.

Before she could voice her concerns, his mouth took hers in a searing kiss, deep, seductive, hotter than hot, dragging her back into oblivion. Nothing existed but Oliver and the way he made her feel. His hands and mouth brought her back up to full arousal. Every part of her was straining for release. She felt achy, empty, needy. Oliver sank the fingers of one hand in her tousled hair, meeting her gaze, his eyes hot with desire. He moved to her and, as she felt him poised for the first time, her hands instinctively grasped at him.

'Relax, Chloe.' His voice was hoarse. He teased kisses at the corners of her mouth, his tongue tip stroking her bottom lip. 'Trust me.'

Slowly, so slowly, he entered her. She felt the unfamiliar pressure. It went on and on as he pressed inexorably forward. Her breaths were coming in ragged gasps, her heart racing madly. For a moment he paused, but before she could tense or prepare herself, he thrust forward again, firmer, surer. The pressure intensified and she felt a sense of impossible fullness. She'd expected pain but there was nothing more than a brief sting before it was gone.

He paused to allow her body to accommodate him. 'Are you OK, babe?'

'Yes,' she managed, although 'OK' didn't seem to cover the magnitude of it.

'Is it uncomfortable for you?'

She shook her head in response to his rough, raw question. The sensations were amazing. His own breathing was as ragged as her own, then he groaned, his hold tightening as he began to move, slowly at first, and then with less restraint. The friction was exquisite. Her fingers dug into the slick flesh of his back. Sobbing, unable to help herself, she curled around him, her hips rising to match his rhythm. Oh, this was fantastic! She loved it. She wanted more. And something far greater than she had already experienced was clamouring inside her.

'Please, Oliver. Please…'

Oliver fought to retain control, to go slowly, to make this first time right for Chloe. But it was impossible not to react to the way she responded so naturally and eagerly to him. Her scent, her taste, the feel of her opening to him, accepting him, welcoming him into her body, was the most incredible thing that had ever happened to him. She fitted him like a glove. He couldn't hold on. He had to move. As she clutched at him, pleaded with him, instinctively wrapped her legs round him and tilted her hips, sending him deeper still, she pushed him over the edge. His control snapping, he upped the tempo, unable to hold back any more. He bound her to him and gave himself up to the unbeliev-able bliss of making love with Chloe MacKinnon. She met and matched his every demand, crying out as he took her higher and higher, until the moment when she flew with him over the pre-cipice, freefalling into the abyss as her release triggered his and unimaginable pleasure shot him spiralling into oblivion.

He had no idea how long it was before he managed to stir himself. He had to be crushing her. Keeping her with him, he carefully rolled them to the side, tightening his hold, needing her close. Always. He had to be dead. He couldn't breathe, his heart was thundering far too fast. Only it wasn't enough. Not nearly enough. For ever wouldn't be enough with Chloe.

Forcing his eyes open, he focused on her flushed face, wiping tears from her cheeks with unsteady fingers. 'Chloe, are you all right? Did I hurt you?'

'No. Not at all. It was… Wow!' A naughty smile sparked her green eyes and curved lips rosy and swollen from his kisses. 'I loved it,' she admitted with a shy laugh. 'Can we do it again?'

Ecstatic, he hugged her and gave a mock groan. 'Help me, I've created an insatiable monster!'

'If you don't want to, I understand.'

'What?' Alerted by the uncertainty in her voice, he rolled them over, cupping her face in his hands. 'Not want to? Are you crazy?'

She bit her lip, making him want to do the same, to taste her again—all over. 'I just thought…'

'Thought once would be enough? Hell no, babe. You can unthink that idea. No way am I ever going to have my fill of you or do all the things I want to do with you.'

* * *

Oliver's words fired new arousal through a body she thought must surely be sated. She couldn't believe she was here with him, that after so many years of locking her sensual side away, Oliver had breezed into her life and so easily broken down the walls of her prison—a prison she hadn't even consciously known existed. Now she knew what she had been missing, but she also knew it wasn't sex per se, it was Oliver himself. She wanted to travel this erotic journey with him for ever.

'Don't move,' he instructed, rolling off her.

'I don't think I could.'

Smiling, she watched as he left the room, presumably to dispose of the condom. She closed her eyes, trying to capture and relive every moment of the most earth-shattering experience of her life. She felt exhilarated, charged, buzzing with life and yet deliciously spent. Her eyes opened as Oliver came back into the room, unselfconscious about his nakedness, and she revelled in being able to look at him in all his naked glory. He was superb. When he knelt on the bed beside her and she realised what he was going to do, she tensed, feeling embarrassed.

Leaning down, he kissed her. 'Let me take care of you, babe.'

A blush stained her cheeks and she closed her eyes, surrendering to him as he used a warm, wet flannel to wash between her thighs. She felt tender, but not unpleasantly so. When he had finished, he surprised her again, lifting her up in his arms and carrying her from the room.

'Where are we going?' she murmured, feeling sleepy.

'I've run a warm bath for you. I don't want you getting stiff and sore.'

Touched by his kindness, she pressed a kiss to his cheek. He set her on her feet beside the bath, cupping her face to bestow a lingering kiss on her lips.

'You get in. I won't be a minute, then I'll scrub your back!'

Smiling, Chloe pinned up her hair and lowered herself into the fragrant bubble bath, the lavender scent relaxing her. Oliver soon returned and slipped into the bath behind her, wrapping his arms around her. For a while she enjoyed resting back against his chest, disinclined to talk. As the water began to cool, Oliver reached for the sponge, soaped it, and took his time working over every inch of her.

'What about my turn?' she complained when he rose and stepped out of the bath.

'Next time.' The devilish smile he sent her as he shook out a towel and held it ready for her made her glow inside with renewed desire. 'I have other plans for you now.'

When he led her back to the bedroom, she discovered he had changed the sheets and again felt a mixture of embarrassment and gratitude for his thoughtfulness. She gasped as he tipped her onto the bed and followed her down, relishing the feeling that this was Oliver let off the leash of the self-control he had maintained until now. He was an amazing man and it hit her for the first time that she'd fallen completely in love with him. Oh, hell. But she didn't have time to fret over the revelation because Oliver's hands and mouth were taking her back to paradise.

In the days that followed, Chloe spent every spare moment she could with Oliver—and every night with him in his bed or hers. Lauren and Kate had noticed the difference in her, claiming she was glowing. Oliver was certainly teaching her things she had never imagined and she was a more than willing pupil, growing in confidence to explore his body and give him pleasure in return.

As she waited for her next patient to arrive, she couldn't stop her mind drifting to Oliver. It always did. The last month had changed her life. *Oliver* had changed her life. She had never been so happy, never felt so free, so content, so whole. But she was scared it wouldn't last. Nothing had been said about any kind of future. Oliver had never discussed his plans for when this contract ended or his flat lease expired, and he had never said how he felt about her, not in words, even while he loved her with his body. She had been equally careful not to betray her own feelings for him, but she very much feared she had given Oliver more than her body. She had given him her heart and her soul.

She had gone into this with her eyes open, so she had no one to blame but herself for falling in love with him—something she had claimed she would never do. But until Oliver, she had never known what love was. Now she did...and it just might break her heart.

CHAPTER NINE

'A QUICK word before you go out to your house calls?'

Oliver looked round at Nick Tremayne's words, halting on his way towards the front entrance of the surgery. 'Of course.'

Puzzled by the request, wondering what Nick wanted to talk to him about, Oliver followed the older man to his consulting room and closed the door.

'Sit down, Oliver.' The senior partner's relaxed manner and rare smile eased Oliver's wariness. 'You're probably aware there are changes afoot in the practice,' Nick began. 'My daughter, Lucy, headed up the plans for expansion before she went on maternity leave. When the alterations are finished we'll have a broader capability to treat minor injuries, plus there will be X-ray facilities and a plaster room. Various other services will be more in-house, including Lauren having a better physiotherapy space to see more patients here.'

'Everyone's very excited about the new facilities,' Oliver agreed.

'Good, good. The workload is continuing to increase for us all, and not just during the tourist season. Initially, your contract was temporary, but your experience suits our needs and will benefit us even more when the expansion is complete.' The older man paused, his gaze assessing as he sat forward and rested his elbows on the desk. 'How would you feel about staying on in Penhally Bay? You've fitted in here, the patients like and trust you, and the staff find you a pleasure to work with. Lucy may not come back to work full time for some time, and Dragan would like to be flexible and reduce his hours when Melinda has their baby. Even with Gabriel Devereux coming over from France for a year in the autumn, we'll need another doctor. We've discussed things, Oliver—myself, Lucy, Dragan and Adam—and we'd like to offer you a full-time post and a junior partnership.'

He felt dumbstruck! When he had first decided to come back to Cornwall, he had hoped to settle down, and the opportunity to stay on permanently suited him down to the ground. Possibilities ran through his mind. Part of him wanted to accept Nick's offer on the spot, knowing he had finally found a place to call home, one that offered the kind of community-based medicine he loved. But another part of him urged patience and caution. He needed to share this with Chloe, to have some sense of what the future held in store for them, and if he had a chance with her long term. If Chloe didn't want him, he wasn't sure he could stay here, to see her, work with her but not touch her and be with her.

For the first time in his life he was in love. He had laid himself bare to Chloe, was totally vulnerable in a way he had never been before. Physically, things just got better and better between them, and she was an avid learner, eager and enthusiastic to experience everything. Emotionally, he felt on shaky ground. For him it was serious. But he had no clue about Chloe's feelings. She had never spoken of them, had never asked about his own. Neither had she asked him about his plans. So many times he had wanted to tell her he loved her but he had held back, scared of her rejection.

Old hurts and doubts nagged at him and he couldn't help but remember the way he had been used so often before. He had never been so uncertain, or so dependent on another person for his happiness, his very existence. Did Chloe see beyond the playboy image to the person he was inside? Could she get over her past and come to love him? He needed answers before he could give Nick a decision.

'Think about it and let me know in a few days,' Nick said now, clearly taking his silence for reticence.

'I will. Thank you, Nick. I'm overwhelmed—but delighted.' Rising to his feet, he shook his boss's hand. 'I just need to be sure of a couple of things before saying one hundred per cent yes.'

A knowing glint appeared in Nick's eyes. 'I understand.'

As he headed out to complete his house calls, Oliver already knew what he wanted. To accept the position, to put down roots in Penhally and make a life with Chloe. To love her, marry her and cherish her. For ever. What would she say when he told her he loved her? Could she care for him as he did for her? Or was he making a mistake in pinning all hopes for the future on her?

'How did the barbecue go?' Chloe asked when she met up with Kate for a quick cup of tea before the final antenatal clinic of the day began.

'It was good.' Kate smiled, helping herself to one of Hazel's home-made biscuits. 'I have to say that Gabriel Devereux, the French doctor, is absolutely *gorgeous*! Dark skin, dark hair, dark eyes. Charm personified. And that accent!'

Chloe smiled. 'Sounds like you're smitten.'

'Unfortunately I'm fifteen or twenty years too old.' Kate chuckled. 'Lucky Lauren, though, having him as a neighbour when he arrives for his year's placement. He loved the Manor House and Nick is making the arrangements for the long-term let.'

'That's good. And what about Jem? Was everything all right?' Chloe asked, concealing how much she had worried about Kate and her son attending Nick's welcoming event for the French GP.

Sitting back in her chair, propping her feet up, Kate looked thoughtful. 'It actually went well. Nick has always known Jem, of course, just not that he's his father,' she explained, lowering her voice even though the staffroom was empty. 'At one point Jem fell over, grazing his knee, and it was Nick who took him indoors to bathe it. I was desperate to go, too, but thought it best to leave well alone. Neither of them said anything but, with at least four other doctors in attendance, I took it as a step forward that Nick wanted to do it himself.'

Chloe hoped Kate was right. It would be good if Nick did come round. Even if he decided not to publicly claim Jem as his son, he could have a friendly relationship with the boy, be an influence in his life as a role model. And she knew Kate would be happy if her own friendship with Nick could return to its former footing, even if her love ultimately remained unrequited.

'How about you and the lovely Oliver?' Kate queried, her eyes twinkling.

Fighting a blush, Chloe thought again of how special he was, how her life had changed because of him. 'It's good. More than good.'

'Why do I sense a but?' Kate sat forward again, a frown creasing her brow. 'What's worrying you, my love?'

'We've just not talked about anything. You know, whatever this is between us. Not beyond taking things a day at a time. I'm terrified he'll move on soon and this brief interlude will be over,' she admitted, her stomach tightening.

'Oh, Chloe. Perhaps Oliver is being cautious because he knows what a big step this is for you,' she suggested, and it was Chloe's turn to frown as she considered her friend's words. 'This is new for him, too. Maybe he needs to hear how *you* feel.'

Chloe thought over what Kate had said as she returned to her room and prepared to greet her first patient of the afternoon.

If only she had some idea how Oliver felt about her, if he planned to stay, she might have the courage to take that extra step and confess how much she loved him.

Never willing to stint on patient care, Oliver forced himself to set his thoughts about his own future aside, but he longed to return to the surgery and see Chloe. The afternoon seemed to drag, but he was soon on his final home visit.

Edith Jones, one of Lucy's patients, lived in a bungalow in Polkerris Road. In her seventies, Edith had endured a tough year. On top of her heart problems and suffering a minor stroke, she had fallen in her home and split her kneecap in two. Since she had returned home from the hospital after initial rehabilitation, the district nurses and a GP visited her regularly, and Lauren was involved in her care, helping her remain as mobile as possible. Oliver had visited Edith a couple of times and was thankful the elderly lady was maintaining Lucy's original advice to change her diet and reduce her salt intake.

'Anything else I can do for you today, Edith?' he asked, packing away his things, satisfied with the results of his examination.

'No. Thank you, Dr Oliver.' She sent him a gentle smile. 'It's a bit of a struggle, but I'm coping, and everyone is very kind. I'm relieved to be able to stay in my own home with my own things around me. Sarah Pearce, my neighbour, is an angel. And I have my cat for company.'

'Call any time if there is anything you need.'

Reassured that Edith was settled, he took his leave. The journey back to the surgery was short and, when he pulled his four-by-four into the car park he saw Lauren getting out of her Renault.

'Hi, Lauren,' he greeted her, balancing his pile of patient notes and his medical bag while locking the door.

'Hello, Oliver.'

'I've just seen Edith Jones. She seems to be doing well.'

Walking with him towards the entrance, Lauren nodded. 'Yes, she is. I'm going in twice a week at the moment.'

They walked into the reception area to be greeted by Sue, the head receptionist. Oliver smiled and set his notes down on the counter for them to be filed away, then accepted the bundle of phone messages Sue handed him.

'Thank you. Anything urgent, Sue?' he asked, flicking through them.

'No, I don't think so. I do have one urgent call for you, though, Lauren,' she continued, handing over the message. 'Can you call back straight away?'

Lauren frowned at the note. 'Of course. I'll do it now.'

'Vicky is here—she said she was meeting you. She's upstairs, talking with Chloe,' Sue explained.

'I'm going up,' Oliver told Lauren, eager to see Chloe himself. 'I'll let Vicky know you're back.'

'Thanks, Oliver.'

Filled with urgency and a sense of purpose, Oliver left his medical bag and his phone messages in his consulting room then headed for the stairs. At the top, he rounded the corner. Chloe's door was open, but as he heard her and Vicky talking he hesitated outside, frozen to immobility, unable to believe what he was hearing. Blindly, he put out a hand to brace himself, feeling as if his heart was being dug out of his chest with a blunt spoon, leaving him bleeding and battered.

'Is that beard rash on your neck?' Vicky grinned, perching on the desk and leaning closer.

'No.' Chloe fought a blush, determined to hide the truth from Vicky. It was just as well she couldn't see the other places on her body that carried the faint mark of the delicious caress of Oliver's stubbled jaw. 'I was in the sun too long.'

Vicky's grin widened. 'Sure you were! So you and Oliver

are finally doing the wild thing, like I told you to. I knew my plan would work. Having him around for a few weeks was bound to liven up your boring sex life.'

'Thanks.' Her ironic riposte was lost on Vicky.

'What's the stud muffin like in bed? I wouldn't mind finding out for myself when you've finished with him…if he sticks around long enough.'

Chloe's hands clenched to fists in her lap as she tried to hide her anger, wishing Lauren would hurry back and rescue her from this torture. The very thought of Oliver with anyone else twisted her insides with pain and jealousy. She liked Vicky…usually. The woman wasn't spiteful, but she was incredibly tactless, leaping in without thinking. No way was Chloe going to leave herself or Oliver open to Vicky's brand of loose talking. And no way did she want Vicky anywhere near Oliver.

'You haven't been stupid enough to fall in love with him, have you, Chloe?' Vicky continued, flicking her fringe—today her hair was green—away from her eyes.

'Of course not,' she lied.

'Well, that's a relief. We all know he's not that kind of man, so it's no use you starting to think wedding bells or anything. That's why he was so perfect for your summer fling.'

'So you said.' Chloe ducked her head to hide her hurt, wanting to yell that Vicky had no idea what kind of man Oliver was. She knew there was no point in explaining, the other girl would never understand how wrong she was. 'Let's forget it, Vicky. It's not important.'

She just wanted Vicky to go. She knew how sensitive Oliver was about people falsely labelling him as a playboy and she was disappointed and cross with Vicky for doing the same thing. She wanted to protect Oliver, to stand up for him, but at the same time she didn't want Vicky spreading rumours and gossip around Penhally about her relationship with Oliver. And she certainly wasn't going to confide to Vicky how she truly felt about him, not until she had told Oliver himself and knew what his plans were and if she stood any chance with him. Vicky knew nothing of her past and would never comprehend what a huge step she had taken in trusting Oliver and finding love with him. It wasn't something she wanted talked about or mocked, however well meaning the teasing might be.

Oliver leaned against the wall, a tight band around his chest preventing him from breathing. Something inside him died and a void opened up. A dark, cold void where just moments ago there had been hope and love and the feeling that maybe this once he had met someone who saw beyond the playboy exterior. He had thought Chloe was different. Apparently not. He stepped into the room, bitter hurt and betrayal swirling inside him, mingling with anger at himself for being such a fool and at Chloe for not being all he had thought she was.

He had tried not to worry that Chloe had said nothing about her feelings, had not wanted to spoil the perfection of their days and nights together by pressing her too soon, by revealing his love for her. He had worried that she might never get beyond her past, and yet he had still gone ahead and laid himself bare to her, committing himself body and soul, leaving himself more vulnerable than ever before.

That Chloe had discussed him with her friends, had been using him as a temporary playboy for some sex education and a holiday fling, hurt more than he believed possible. He was devastated. All his dreams and plans, fledgling ones that had taken real flight after Nick's offer earlier, now crumbled to dust around him.

In the moment before Chloe or Vicky noticed his presence, he drank in the sight of the woman he had so wanted to believe in but who had hurt him beyond bearing. She glanced round then, shock and guilt in her expressive eyes when her gaze met his.

'Oliver! I—'

'Vicky, Lauren is waiting for you downstairs,' he interrupted, somehow managing to force the words past the tightness in his throat.

'Oops! Didn't see you there.' With an irritating giggle, Vicky slid off the edge of Chloe's desk. 'Thanks. I'll see you later.'

A tense silence followed her departure. Feeling as if the floor had been pulled out from under him, he thrust his hands in his pockets and forced himself to look at Chloe. 'Nick offered me a permanent job in Penhally.'

He watched as her face lost colour and renewed shock widened moss-green eyes. Clearly this wasn't the pleasant surprise he'd wanted it to be and she'd meant what she'd said to Vicky—she didn't love him, had never expected more than a few nights in his bed before he moved on.

'You're thinking of staying here?'

'Of course, that doesn't fit in with your plans, does it, babe?' Hurt brought a sarcastic edge to his voice. 'You and Vicky had it all figured out. I was a not entirely repulsive *stud* you thought you could use to satisfy your curiosity about sex for a night or two because it wouldn't matter to me.'

Chloe stared at Oliver in horror. The icy chill of his voice was matched by the expression in his eyes, eyes devoid of their normal life and warmth.

'That's not—'

'I heard what you said.'

'Oliver!' Hazel's urgent call from the direction of the landing prevented Chloe making a rebuttal. 'We have an emergency outside. Can you come?'

'Of course.' He cast Chloe one searing look before turning away. 'I'm done here.'

The finality of the words cut Chloe to the quick. 'But—'

Chloe watched through a film of tears as Oliver strode away, his footsteps retreating down the stairs as he followed Hazel. Slumping against her desk, her whole body shaking in reaction, Chloe wrapped her arms around herself. Damn Vicky. Just how much of their conversation had Oliver heard? It must have sounded bad. And on top of that, instead of responding with the joy and hope she felt at the thought of Oliver staying, the shock and confusion of the last moments had made her reaction slow and lukewarm.

What was she going to do? So inexperienced at this kind of thing, she had made a mess of everything. Because of her past, she hadn't believed she could be happy, that what she felt for Oliver was real, that it could work. Had not believed he could love her. But his pain had been obvious. She would never forget the look in his eyes. The knowledge that he now believed she had used him stung.

'Chloe, what the hell is going on?' Lauren demanded, rushing into the room and closing the door behind her.

Tears trickled down her cheeks and her voice shook. 'Oliver's gone. It's over.'

'Vicky told me what happened. She's an idiot.' Lauren handed her a tissue and slid an arm around her shoulder. 'So will you be if you let Oliver go. Damn it, Chloe! You have to go after him.'

'No.' A sob escaped. She thought she had known what pain was like but this was worse, much worse. 'I can't. He'd never believe me now.'

Lauren cursed. 'I was there when he followed Hazel down-stairs. He was devastated. I've never seen anyone look so broken. You love him, Chloe, I know you do. Don't let it end like this. It's too important, for both of you. He doesn't know what Vicky is like, he didn't understand you were trying to protect him from gossip. He's not a mind-reader. You have to explain.'

'I've been too scared to tell him I love him.' Chloe's throat closed and her chest crushed with hurt. 'Now it's too late. I let him down.'

'*Tell* him.'

'What if he won't talk to me?' she whispered through her tears, scared she had driven Oliver away for good.

'You won't know until you try. Make him listen,' Lauren advised. 'He's hurting now because he loves you. You love him. What have you got to lose?'

Nothing, Chloe realised as her friend left her alone to think. She had already lost everything that mattered to her. A fierce mix of need and hurt and anger swirled inside her. She was angry with herself for handling things so badly, angry with Vicky for interfering, angry and disappointed that Oliver hadn't given her the chance to explain. It hurt that he hadn't believed in her enough. But why should he? She'd never told him how she felt, had taken everything he had given her these last weeks but had still doubted. After what he had overheard, followed by her reaction, what else was he to think?

Lauren was right. She was the only one who could change that. Oliver was worth fighting for. She gathered up her things and hurried down the stairs, upset to discover that Oliver had left. The emergency had been a suspected heart attack and he had gone along in the ambulance to St Piran with the critically ill patient. No one could tell when he might be back.

Unwilling to hang around the surgery, she went home to shower and change her clothes. After feeding the cats, she paced her small living room. Several times she phoned Oliver's flat but there was no reply, and his mobile was switched off. When her phone rang, she jumped and rushed to answer, hoping it was Oliver, swallowing her disappointment when she discovered it was not. It was Kate.

'Are you all right, Chloe? What's going on with you and Oliver?'

'I don't know.' Her voice trembled with tears. 'He overheard me talking to Vicky this afternoon. She can be so persistent and thoughtless. I told her a few fibs. I was trying to stop her gossiping, but now Oliver thinks I have just been using him. It isn't true!'

'I know that, my love. So will Oliver when he's calmed down,' Kate reassured her, but Chloe knew it wasn't that simple.

'He told me that Nick had offered him a permanent post. Oh, Kate, I was so shocked, so stunned to discover he had heard me and Vicky, that I reacted badly. I didn't get the chance to explain, and now he believes there's nothing between us, that I don't care. And that's my fault, too, because I was too scared to tell him.'

A heartfelt sigh from Kate increased her anxiety. 'He's going, Chloe. I was here at the surgery when he came back from the hospital fifteen minutes ago. He told Nick he didn't want the job, that there was nothing for him to stay for.'

'No!'

'Go to him, my love. It doesn't matter who is more at fault, you are both hurting and you need each other. If you don't talk to him, you will always regret it,' Kate counselled, reinforcing Lauren's advice. 'Make it right, Chloe…before it's too late.'

Knowing there was a wealth of meaning behind Kate's words, empathising with her friend's difficult situation with Nick, the man she had loved for so long, Chloe made her decision.

Oliver tossed clothes into his bags, trying to use anger to mask the bitter lance of terrible pain. How could he have been so stupid? Chloe wasn't different at all. Like everyone else, she had seen the outer package, the reputation, and not the man inside. His gut ached at the knowledge she had used him as some kind of sex tutor. And he would never forget the look of shock on her face when he had told her he was staying. Clearly she didn't want him. He had read everything wrong and now there was nothing for him in Penhally Bay.

A furious pounding on the door had his head snapping up. He hesitated. He wasn't on duty. Indeed, he had a few days off to decide if he even wanted to see out his contract here. But what if someone was in trouble? Hell. He ran a hand through his hair and stalked towards the door. Throwing it open, he froze when he saw who waited outside. Chloe. Her hand, raised to knock again, fell to her side. Before he could react, she pushed past him.

'What do you want, Chloe, another quick tumble in bed before the playboy leaves town?' He hated himself for the words and tried to close his mind to the hurt clouding her green eyes.

'No. That wouldn't be enough.' She folded her arms across her chest and fixed him with a glare. 'I'm here because you didn't give me a chance to explain and I'm not going to let you judge me and leave without me saying my piece.'

Unwanted amusement and affection welled inside him at her bravado. He'd never seen her so riled before. It was cute. No, he— Before he could formulate his thoughts and raise his defences again, she launched into her attack.

'Do you seriously think, with my background and having waited until the age of twenty-seven, that I would suddenly turn into some kind of sexpot who is going to sleep with anyone for the sake of it? Yes, Vicky made some stupid comment when she found out you were interested in me that I should go for it. But that's Vicky. She doesn't know about my past. She certainly doesn't know me if she thought I could ever do such a thing.' She paused a moment, dragging in a lungful of air. 'And neither can you if you believe it, even for a moment. I didn't come on to you, chase you. You courted me. And it was only when I came to know you, to like you, to trust you, that I began to wonder if maybe you were someone special, someone who made it worth my while to confront things that terrified me and open myself up to experiences I had shut out of my life because I was so scared. You think I would have just jumped into bed with anyone?'

She was shaking with rage and hurt. All the fight went out of him as every word she said hit home and he acknowledged how badly he had behaved, how horribly he had treated her. Yes, he did know her better. He just hadn't allowed himself to believe it could be true that he had found his perfect soulmate, that she could ever come to love him back, that there could be a happy ever after. Just when it had all been falling into place, everything had been shaken up and he had allowed his own in-securities to get the better of him, to believe the worst of her.

'Chloe…' He tried to swallow past the lump in his throat and find his voice. 'I'm sorry.'

'So am I.'

Tears shimmered on long sooty lashes as he closed the gap between them. 'I was so dumb.'

'Me, too.'

'Can you forgive me, babe? Please?'

'Oliver—'

He rested the fingers of one hand over her lips, not wanting her to reject him as he deserved, needing to say his own piece while he had the chance. 'I should never have paid heed to what I heard. I was just so stunned, so hurt when you told Vicky you didn't love me.'

'Vicky means well, but she's the biggest gossip in Penhally, Oliver, and she has zero tact. I didn't want her telling all and sundry our private business. I was angry with her for judging you, for being so shallow, but I knew she would never listen, never understand, so I let her ramble on. No way was I going to tell Vicky, of all people, about my feelings—not when I hadn't even had the courage to tell you.'

'Chloe,' he murmured, stepping closer, a glimmer of hope challenging the darkness inside him. 'When I came back to Cornwall, I was jaded, fed up with people using me because of the family name, the money, my so-called playboy lifestyle. Sure, I liked to have a good time, to enjoy myself, but no one saw *me*. The person inside. Not until you. I was drawn to you from the first and the more I came to know you, the more I knew you were special, and I dared to allow myself to believe.' He cupped her face, breathing in her fresh apple scent. 'Nick sprang the junior partnership on me and immediately I had all these plans and wanted to share them with you. But I had no idea how you felt. When I heard you talking and it seemed to have all been some grand scheme for a fling between us, I let the hurt and fear get in the way of my common sense and all I knew about you. I was scared because I thought I had been a fool to think someone like you could possibly care about someone like me.'

'Someone like you?' she challenged, her own hands lifting to grasp his wrists. 'A fantastic, caring doctor, adored by his patients, young and old, male and female? Someone like you, who is good and kind, funny and intelligent, selfless and giving? Someone like you who saw *me* when no one else had, and who cared enough to wait, to gain my trust, to spend so much time getting me through the scary moments and awakening me to all I was missing by not setting the past behind me where it belongs? Someone like you, who changed my life…who made me really feel alive for the first time? That someone like you?'

'Yeah.' Love and desire glowed inside him at the sincerity of her words.

'Oliver, I don't care about your bank balance. I don't care about Fawkner Yachts. It wouldn't matter to me who your family were as long as they loved you and were proud of you. I'm proud of you. And I love you. I should have told you before, but I was scared, too. Scared you would leave soon and I'd never see you again. Scared none of this meant to you what it did to me. You stole my heart, you made me believe in romance and love and for ever. You even made me like sex,' she added with a shy laugh, a blush staining her cheeks.

'Chloe…'

Her eyes full of vulnerability, she stepped back a couple of paces and pulled the tie holding the fabric of her floaty dress together. She let it drop, revealing barely-there silk and lace bra and panties. Every part of him sprang to attention. OK. Any moment now he would remember how to breathe. That or pass out. Dear God…

'I've never seduced a man before.'

He filled his lungs on a ragged gasp. 'You're doing one hell of a good job,' he managed, his voice hoarse with love and admiration and desire.

'Am I?'

'Oh, yeah.' Given how hard he was and how close to embarrassing himself. 'Don't move.'

He reached for the phone, his fingers shaking as he felt for the keys and dialled a number, his gaze never leaving Chloe's.

'Nick? It's Oliver Fawkner. If the offer for the junior partnership still stands, I'd like to accept. Thank you. Yes, I'm sorry about that, it was a misunderstanding. I've just discovered that I have everything to stay for. All I'll ever need is right here in Penhally Bay.'

As he replaced the receiver, he saw joy dance in Chloe's beautiful green eyes, along with a whole host of feelings that mirrored his own. To think he had been so foolish to risk throwing this away. 'Now, you said something about seducing me.'

'Yes. That.'

'Don't let me stop you,' he invited, his fingertips brushing across the rounded swell of her breasts over the top edges of her bra, enjoying the tremor that rippled through her.

'I was kind of hoping you might take over at this point.'

'I don't know. You're doing so well.'

'Really?'

'Don't you know you had me on my knees from the moment we met?'

She shook her head, looking shy yet bold, sexy yet uncertain as her fingers began to undo the buttons of his shirt. 'I only know you didn't give up on me, didn't let my past and my fears chase you away.'

He moaned as she freed his shirt, leaned forward and closed her mouth over one sensitive nipple. Not wanting to be left out, he deftly unhooked her bra and tossed it away, filling his palms with her firm, full, soft flesh.

'How about we do the seducing together?' he suggested hoarsely.

'Good idea.'

'We'll do everything together, Chloe, for the rest of our lives. I'll do all I can to make you happy and I'll love you for ever. If you'll let me.'

'Yes.' She whimpered as his thumbs brushed over taut nipples. 'I will. If you'll let me love you for ever, too.'

'I think I can manage that.'

Her fingers fumbled with the fastening of his jeans. 'Starting now?'

'Hell, yes!' He kissed her, long and hard and deep. 'What say we shock Vicky and make it another wedding for Penhally before the year is out?'

'Lauren is right. There definitely must be something in the water!'

He nipped her earlobe. 'Is that a yes?'

'Of course it's a yes!'

'I already have a present for you,' he told her with a teasing smile, thinking of the jet-ski he'd ordered.

Green eyes sparkled with mischief as she looked at him. 'Funny. I have a present for you, too. It's at home. I hid it in the spare room. It's for your birthday, but I was going to give it to you if you left…to remember me by.'

'As if I could ever forget you.' He groaned, pulling her close. 'And I'm never leaving, babe.' As curious as he was about what she had bought him, amazed and touched that she had done such a thing, he had other things on his mind right now. 'Presents can wait until later.'

'Whatever did you have in mind?'

Laughing, he swung her up in his arms and carried her to the bedroom. He set her back on her feet, grimacing when he saw her pained expression as she looked at his half-packed luggage.

'Like I said, I was dumb.'

'You can still pack.'

He froze at her words. 'What do you mean?'

'Your lease here runs out any day.' Shy invitation shone in her eyes. 'I was thinking… Maybe you'd care to move in with me?'

'I'd love to. And down the line, when we decide about a family, we can find a new home together that we can grow into. With the cats, of course.'

'Perfect.'

'No. You're perfect.' He tipped her on to the bed and stripped off the rest of his clothes. 'Do you think, knowing you—and your background—that I ever would have embarked on a relationship with you if all I had wanted was a quick, meaningless tumble before I moved on again? You're not a quick tumble kind of woman, Chloe. If I'd only wanted one night, I would never have touched you. I would have walked away. But I came here to settle down, to meet the right woman for me, and

I soon knew you were the one. You are a forever kind of woman. My forever woman. It's happened quickly, but I love you. And I've never said that to anyone before. I know this is all new to you. If you need time to be sure, that's fine, I understand. But I'm only going to love you more each day.'

Tears filled her eyes, threatening to spill past her lashes. 'I am sure. I love you, too. So much. I just can't believe I'm enough for you.'

'Babe, you are everything.' He joined her on the bed, dipping his head to steal a hot kiss. 'And it'll be my pleasure to prove it to you every day for the rest of our lives.'

She wriggled out of her panties. 'Starting now.' It was half question, half demand, her voice throaty with arousal.

'This very second.'

He fulfilled his promise, as he planned to fulfil all his promises to her, now and for all the years that lay ahead of them. How could he be this lucky? He was the happiest man alive, and if he had his way, Chloe was going to be the most satisfied woman in Penhally Bay. Hell, the whole world!

Linking his fingers with hers, holding her gaze, he united them, starting them on their journey to paradise together, joining not just their bodies, but their hearts and their souls…for ever.

* * * *

BRIDES OF PENHALLY BAY

Let us whisk you away to this Cornish coastal town – to a place where hearts are made whole.

Read on for a sneak preview from
Their Miracle Baby by Caroline Anderson
– the ninth book in the
BRIDES OF PENHALLY BAY series.

THEIR MIRACLE BABY

by

Caroline Anderson

DADDY!'

'Hello, pickle!' Mike scooped Sophie up into his arms and whirled her round, their laughter ringing round the yard and echoing off the old stone walls of the barn, bringing a lump to her throat.

These two adored each other, and now both their faces were lit up with a joy so infectious Fran couldn't help but smile.

'How's my favourite girl today?' he asked, hugging her tight and looking down into her beaming face.

'I'm fine— Daddy, where's Fran? I've got something really special to show her— Fran! Look!' she yelled, catching sight of her and waving madly.

She wriggled out of his arms, running across and throwing herself at Fran. She caught her little stepdaughter, hugging her close and laughing, kissing her bright, rosy cheek and holding out her hand for the little box Sophie was thrusting at her eagerly.

'It's a model—I made it at school!' she confided in a stage whisper. 'It's Daddy milking a cow—see, here's Amber, and this is Daddy, and this is the cluster…'

She pointed underneath the misshapen reddish blob that could just conceivably have been a cow, and there was a thing like a mangled grey spider stuck on her underside. She supposed if the blob could be Amber, then the spider could be a milking machine cluster. Why not? And as for Mike…

'I'm going to give it to him for his birthday,' she went on still whispering loud enough to wake the dead. 'We've got to wrap it. Have you got paper?'

Fran smiled and put the lid back on the box. 'I'm sure we've got paper,' she whispered back. 'It's lovely. Well done darling. I'm sure he'll be really pleased.'

A flicker of doubt passed over Sophie's earnest little face. 'Do you think so? Amber was really hard to make.'

'I'm sure, but you've done it beautifully. He'll be so pleased. He loves everything you make for him. It makes him feel *really* special.'

Sophie brightened, her confidence restored, and whirling round she ran back to her beloved father and grabbed his hand. 'I want to go and see the cows— Oh, Brodie!' she said breaking away again and dropping to her knees to cuddle the delighted collie who was lying on her back, grinning hideously and wagging her tail fit to break it. 'Hello, Brodie,' she crooned, bending right down and letting the dog wash her face with meticulous attention.

'Sophie, you mustn't let her do that!' Kirsten protested, but Sophie ignored her mother, laughing and hugging the dog while Brodie licked and licked and licked for England.

'Yeah, not your face, it's not a good idea,' Mike chipped in, backing Kirsten up simply because he just did. It was one of the many things Fran loved about him, the way he defended Sophie's mother's decisions to their daughter even if he didn't agree, and then discussed it with her rationally when Sophie wasn't around.

The fact that Brodie washed his face whenever it was in reach was neither here nor there! Now he held out his hand to Sophie and pulled her to her feet—and out of range of Brodie's tongue—with a grin.

'Come on, scamp, say goodbye to your mum and then let's go and see the cows. I'm sure they've missed you.'

Missed the treats, no doubt, because the six-year-old always seemed to have her little pockets bulging with pellets of feed, and she'd happily give it to them despite the cows' slippery noses and rough, rasping tongues. Nothing fazed her, and she was deliriously happy trailing round after her father and 'helping' him.

'Fran?' Sophie said, holding out her hand expectantly after they'd waved Kirsten off, but she shook her head. This was their time, precious and special to both of them, and she wouldn't intrude.

'I've got to make supper,' she said with a smile. 'You go with your father and say goodnight to the cows. I'll see you both soon.' And with a little wave she watched them head off towards the field where the cows were grazing, Mike shortening his stride to accommodate his little sprite, Sophie skipping and dancing beside him, chattering nineteen to the dozen while her pale blonde bunches bobbed and curled and flicked around her head.

They went round the corner out of sight, Brodie at their heels, and with a soft sigh Fran went back inside, the little cardboard box containing Mike's present in her hand. She opened the lid and stared down at the little lumps of modelling clay so carefully and lovingly squashed into shape, and her eyes filled. He was so lucky to have her. So very, very lucky.

If only it could happen to them.

They'd come so close—twice now.

It often happened, she'd been told. Miscarriages were common, and her first, three years ago—well, that had just been one of those things, they'd said. It probably wouldn't happen again.

And it hadn't, of course, because she hadn't conceived again, and so they'd undergone endless intrusive and humiliating tests, all of which had proved nothing except that there wasn't any obvious reason why they hadn't had a baby yet.

So they'd gone through the difficult and challenging process of a cycle of IVF, and she'd become pregnant, and then, just like before, she'd lost it.

Not unusual, they were told again, especially with IVF possibly because the embryos weren't always as perfect as they might be with a normally conceived embryo, and this it seemed, was probably what had happened to theirs.

All very logical, but she didn't feel logical about it, because there was nothing wrong with either of them, they just hadn't managed to make a healthy baby yet, and it was tearing her apart.

Looking on the bright side, they hadn't made an unhealthy one either, so if that was why the embryos had both failed, maybe it was for the best.

Small consolation.

Whatever the reason, she'd lost the embryos, and she wasn't sure she had the strength to go through it again. If she had another miscarriage…

And, anyway, they still had Sophie coming to visit them and bringing so much sunshine into their lives. OK, it wasn't like having her own child, but Sophie was gorgeous, and she loved her to bits. Was it greedy to want more?

To want a child of their own who would come home from

chool bubbling with excitement and giving them some little
lob of modelling clay to treasure?

She dragged in a breath, pressing her fist against the little
knot of pain in her chest. Not now. She couldn't think about
it now. Blinking hard, she put the little box in a safe place,
opened the fridge and started pulling things out.

Supper. Practicalities. Forget the rest.

Just like the funny, amazing little present, she had to put
her feelings in a box and put the lid on and put them all away.

It was the only way to survive.

Margaret McDonagh

QUESTIONS & ANSWERS

Would you like to live in the fictional Cornish town of Penhally Bay?

I loved getting to know the community in Penhally Bay and it is certainly a lovely town in a beautiful setting. I'd love to visit often and holiday there, but I'm more of a country girl than a beach person so I don't think I could live there full time.

Did you enjoy writing as part of the *Brides of Penhally Bay* series?

Very much so. It was my first experience of taking part in a continuity series and I learned a great deal. It was fascinating discovering a different way to work, not only with trying to blend in the ongoing storyline that runs through all twelve books, but also starting out in a very different way, having an outline and main characters given to me rather than making them up myself. But Oliver and Chloe soon became very much my own and I love them to pieces.

What was it like working with other authors to create the backdrop to these books?

Writing is usually a solitary occupation, leaving you alone with your doubts and uncertainties, not to mention the worry about meeting that deadline that is looming. Of course, you have your characters for company, but they don't always behave themselves and do what you expect them to! Being part of the continuity also meant that it was necessary to take into account other authors' characters and stories so that everything flowed as seamlessly as possible. So it was a novel experience to work together with other authors to bring Penhally Bay and all the people who live, work and love there to life. I've made some very good friends thanks to Penhally Bay and I feel very blessed and honoured to have been part of this series.

Tell us about a typical day's writing!

There really isn't such a thing as a typical day for me. I can't write a set number of words for a set amount of time a day. I'm very character-driven and the more I get to know my hero and heroine, the more they come to life inside me. Their story unfolds and they lead me on the journey. Some days words gush out and I can write for hours – other days are less productive in terms of word count. But I'm thinking! It's not all work at the keyboard.

How did you first start writing romance novels?

I've always written and it was always my dream to be published. That certainly didn't happen overnight. My first efforts showed promise but were not right for publication, so I went away and wrote short stories, serials and novellas for magazines, learning and, hopefully, growing as a writer. The urge remained to write books, so I decided to have another try. To my delight and amazement, my first Medical™ was accepted. I was on cloud nine and haven't floated down much since then! I'm loving every moment of it and hope to continue for as long as possible. I have so many voices and characters in my head demanding for their stories to be told – and a lot of scrumptious heroes wanting to be let loose, so watch out!

What do you love most about your hero and heroine in *Virgin Midwife, Playboy Doctor*?

I just adore Oliver. I love his compassion and his gentleness. I love his patience with Chloe, his understanding of her. I love his humour and his sexiness and his wicked side! I also love that he's vulnerable. As for Chloe, I love how she has battled to overcome her past, how she's made so much of her life. And I love how she blossoms under Oliver's care, how she faces the very things she fears most and opens herself up to things she never believed she could know and then embraces them. I think Oliver and Chloe are perfect for each other. They complete each other. Alone they are both strong and caring and independent – together they are so much more.

Can we have a sneak preview of your next book...?

My next published book is *Dr Devereux's Proposal*, which is book twelve in this Penhally Bay series. It brings the sexy and gorgeous French doctor, Gabriel Devereux, to town and an instant attraction flares between him and physiotherapist Lauren Nightingale. But they each have issues to face and overcome if they are ever going to have a future together. The next Medical™ I am working on as I write this is set back in my fictional Scottish world of Strathlochan. It tells the story of A&E doctor Annie Webster, who has been a secondary character in previous books. What happens when she comes face to face with the man she once loved? Can she come to terms with the past, the mistakes she made, and will she find she has a future with Nathan after all?